YEAR THREE

2021

Editing by S. Jade Path and The Crimson Wordsmith
Cover Design by Dawn Burdett
Internal Formatting by Ben Thomas

Also available from Black Hare Press

ANNUALS

YEAR ONE
YEAR TWO
YEAR THREE
YEAR FOUR

linktr.ee/blackharepress

Contents

Preface

YEAR THREE IS a culmination of all the stories that have appeared in Dark Moments on the Black Hare Press website and on the BHP Patreon throughout 2021.

Thank you to all the wonderful authors who crafted tales for us this year. To those presented here, in Year Three, and everyone else who published with us in other publications.

We've been helped throughout by family and friends, collaborators, editors, the amazing read team, the group moderators, and a myriad of helpers: we couldn't have done it without you.

Special thanks to our Patreon supporters, especially S. Jade Path, James Aitchison, and Jonathan Stiffy. Take a look at the Patreon-only content and merchandise here—patreon.com/blackharepress—and consider helping us get to the next stage.

And, as always, to our discerning reader: this was all done for you. We hope you enjoyed these tales, and if you did, don't forget to leave a review.

Love & kisses,
Ben & the Black Hare Press Team

The Deluge

by Isaac Menuza

IT HAD BEEN raining since the day Thome left. Not a healthy, nurturing rain, but the type that soaked him to the marrow and corroded his soul. The type of rain that had made a pregnant lover appear so sorrowful in the rearview mirror.

He couldn't have known then that the rain wouldn't stop. That it would flood every lowland. That it would push all the unwanted things—all that couldn't be carried—into overflowing culverts and canals.

The things Thome carried populated this cabin. Not just the cans of food, the camping stove, and the chipped mug from which he slurped bitter coffee. Not just the worn songbook at his feet and neglected guitar in his hands, but also the acid things that nestled in his heart.

He wasn't sure what compelled him to tune this old instrument, how he'd come to be on this stool, plucking lonely notes on loose strings. Those vibrating particles drifted on the rain's arrhythmic percussion, a composition in brokenness.

When the rain started twenty-five years ago, before this beard and before these xylophone ribs, it would have been the sound of a muttering audience that underpinned those modulating notes—an intimate crowd in a bookstore, coffee shop, bar, or gallery in the arts district of some bright-lit city.

His lack of roots was the only thing that saved him when the rains came. He never asked for a family, wouldn't accept one if it was offered. Didn't accept one when it was offered...

Thome cleared phlegm from lungs thick with flotsam and blew a tangle of grey hair from his face. Outside, new rivulets of runoff found their way through the pines and down the slope. The path of new water was nearly as unpredictable as the path of new life; however, once it found its way, it could carve a canyon. In another life, he'd have jotted that lyric down.

An anomalous pattern in the movement outside his window piqued Thome's interest. One of the water's flows careened along a natural gutter toward an animal in the distance—a small bear or a moose calf, maybe. But the movement was odd. At intervals, the animal appeared to evaporate and re-materialise a step closer to the cabin. It was as though the rain was repeatedly washing the creature out of existence.

A trick of the light.

He set his guitar against the clapboard, under tic marks that denoted the months in this shelter.

Whatever the thing was, there weren't many such beasts in this area anymore. Thome cracked the seal of the front door and stepped under the tarp he'd fashioned over the stoop. A coughing fit ignited his lungs.

The animal had closed the distance to an unsettling degree. Only, it wasn't an animal at all, but a man. The stranger continued his bizarre, flickering movement.

"Hullow!" Thome called through a raw throat. This time, the coughing unearthed a reddish ball of mucus that he spat into the waters running past his front step.

No response from the stranger.

This was the first person Thome had seen since coming to the cabin, and the first person he'd tried to interact with in years. When he scavenged the floods, he kept his skiff hidden and avoided human contact. He wished he had a gun—or that he even knew how to shoot.

The stranger was sufficiently close now that Thome would have been able to distinguish his features if not for the hood of the man's drab rain slicker. The stranger was young enough to stand straight and old enough—or stupid enough—to approach an inhabited cabin with confidence. The slicker billowed around his boots, which were covered by water and hardly seemed to be moving at all.

"Can stop right there." It hadn't sounded as tough as he'd hoped. His voice was always more pretty than gruff.

Pretty. That's how Robin had described it while they were sharing a cigarette outside a club in Philly. He'd laughed at her defiant grin, braces reflecting the pink lights that wrapped the wall like barbwire. She'd reached up and rubbed the abundant brown curls sprouting from his scalp. The spark behind her jade eyes only grew brighter as the night wore on. She would always have stood out among the other girls—unexpected pregnancy notwithstanding.

The stranger had halted at the edge of the clearing, beneath the protective boughs of a tall cedar. His face remained hidden in the shade of his hood. Maybe if he moved, some aspect would reveal itself, but he was as still as a sheltered pool.

"What's your business?" Thome asked.

What Thome at first mistook for the gurgle of one of the streams turned out to be a sound originating deep within the shadow of that hood. In time, it formed itself into a word. "Home."

It might have been the first time the stranger spoke the word—working his way around it, over it. His voice was a splash of water rebounding from a cave.

Thome straightened himself and fought against the iron finger scratching at his throat. "This isn't your home. More cabins around if you're lost and need a place."

Dark flows washed against the stranger's calves. "Coming. Home," he said, splitting the syllables in an off-kilter cadence. The tarp over Thome's head whipped in the growing wind and tumbled clods of water into the puddles around him.

The heavy rain made distances fuzzy, blurred the line between solid object and liquid. Once, it seemed that a dark shape wriggled beneath the shallow water around the stranger's feet, but it disappeared before Thome could observe it further.

The stranger drifted closer.

"Just, turn around," Thome said, but the rain swallowed it. "I got a gun inside."

The stranger lifted hands grey as a seaside dawn and pulled his hood back. Thick brown curls soaked up the precipitation. The stranger lifted a smooth face to Thome, regarded him with green eyes—fire behind jade. Runnels dripped from a chin round as river rock. The same type of chin Robin had nibbled under bed covers and caught in her mouth like a fish on bait.

"You…" Thome said.

The stranger worked out a kink in his mouth, wrestled with wet lips that appeared intent on slipping from his face. "Coming home," he said, having found a smoother path around the words.

***

"Please, take off your jacket."

The stranger made no move to do so. Water cascaded from his slicker and pooled on the floor. It looked as though the water sluiced from inside the jacket. The stranger shuffled quietly to the centre of the room, leaving a wet trail behind him.

Thome shut the door on nature's free jazz arrangement, chattering rain against the tarp, wind abrading the pine needles. The stranger gazed at the paint can warming over the stove.

"Coffee?"

The stranger nodded. The rain had plastered the man's thick curls to his face. His skin was cloudy ivory but looked soft as sand. He was young, probably late twenties. The timing worked out.

Don't be stupid. Living alone in the woods had a way of degrading one's faculties, Thome knew. The sheer coincidence of the boy finding him after all these years— after the deluge—it just wasn't possible.

"I'd offer a towel," Thome said while wiping an unloved mug with an equally unloved rag, "but doesn't look like it'd do much good."

He stared at the water that continued to pour from the stranger's slicker. It was as if the rain had suffused the kid, and under the slicker he was nothing but a large droplet.

Thome said, "Can't keep all the water out anyway."

He dipped a rusty ladle into the paint can, then deposited boiling coffee into the stranger's mug.

"Never gave me your name," he said as he handed the cup over.

The stranger didn't look to be listening. His green eyes slid over the modest accommodations, probably taking in the ripped fabric of the cot, the nails and tools piled in the corner, the battery-powered lantern hanging from a crossbeam.

The puddle at the stranger's feet had widened now, a ripple emanating from the centre of the room. He cradled the mug of coffee in his grey hands. A soft grumbling came from beneath the creased material of the stranger's jacket. The way the fabric bunched around the stranger's torso created shadows that shifted across his midsection.

"Guess your stomach does the talking for you, huh? Take a seat. I'll make us some breakfast."

Thome was more surprised at the offer of hospitality than the stranger seemed to be. He wasn't typically the considerate one. It did remind him, though, of a particular morning: him using chopsticks to scramble eggs in a hot skillet, a certain naked girl untangling herself from a fishnet of bedsheets.

"They're fluffier if you scramble them beforehand, you know," she'd told him at the table, harpooning a white and yellow chunk. "Not everything has to happen spontaneously." She took her bite then ran her fork around the edge of her plate. "God, now I sound like my parents."

"Better if we don't talk about your parents," he'd said, rubbing at his chin and the light scratch left by her braces.

The next time he heard from Robin was several months later, when someone from the label managed to get her letter into his hands.

He didn't like to think of his response. It'd been a joke. Or mostly a joke. Like something you say only because it popped into your head, and you thought it was clever. But it had popped into his head, hadn't it?

Maybe you should have scrambled it beforehand, he'd written to her.

No fresh eggs for the stranger, though. Just corned beef hash cooked in the can. He poured roughly half of the steaming contents into his only bowl and set it before the stranger. Thome placed the hot can on an oven mitt and stuck his spoon inside.

"Wasn't expecting company."

The stranger put down his coffee. A slurry spilled from the sleeves of his slicker over the edge of the table.

"You have a name? Or did that wash away too?"

Brighter flames behind jade. The stranger mulled an awkward tongue in his mouth. He made a croaking sound in the back of his throat, popped those wet lips. "B—"

The stranger seemed satisfied, didn't bother to finish the rest. He shoved a mouthful of canned meat in his mouth, tipped his head back, and choked the food down his gullet.

"So that's it, then? Buh? B for short?" Thome took more care with his bite. He blew on it, chewed it thoroughly with aching teeth.

The stranger cocked his head sideways, observing Thome more closely. Maybe he was seeing the unruly hair, or the cuts and bruises on his arms from the fall he took off the roof. Or maybe he heard the semi-solid rattling of Thome's respiration.

Or maybe he'd finally noticed the resemblance.

He's got my eyes but your wanderlust. That's what Robin wrote in her last letter, before the floods got really bad, back when Thome could still find paying gigs—or any gigs at all.

Please, come back. Things are getting bad here.

What would he have done? As it was, he barely survived on his own. He'd been flooded out of shelters. He'd been shot at by roughnecks in a fishing boat. He'd eaten a bad batch of beans and suffered days of continuous delirium. How would he care for Robin and her son?

Brandon.

B.

Their son.

Something was soaking into Thome's shoes. Dark water continued to flow from under B's slicker. The cabin smelled of churned soil, of muck and worms. For some reason, the puddle at Thome's feet cast no reflection. He wouldn't have wanted to look at it anyway.

"You're probably wondering why I left," he said. He coughed into his arm and rubbed a sleeve across his mouth. "I've never met a reason that didn't disappoint me."

B didn't react, not directly. However, he turned his head toward the front of the cabin, turned it far enough that it made Thome squirm. Something scratched against the inside of B's jacket. Thome made a passing note of it, as he had recognised the object of B's attention: His guitar and songbook, moments away from being overtaken by the spreading water.

Thome shot from his chair and retrieved them. Outside, the sky's torrents increased their fervour. Rain splattered the window, assaulted the rooftop.

Thome sloshed through the cabin's interior pool back to his seat. He propped the songbook against the can of hash and set the guitar in his lap. He strummed the open strings.

"As close to tuned as these old ears will allow," he said. There was a seam in B's slicker, open at the collar. Thome couldn't remember it having been there previously. B's mouth opened as if he might say something, but if he did, it blended with the surge of wind against the cabin.

Thome plucked the fifth and sixth strings. He'd always thought of these thicker strings as his anchor, the only thing holding him to this earth.

"Twenty-five years ago, I wrote a song. I never played it live. Only ever intended it for one audience. A song changes every time you play it, just by context and feeling. The audience, they change it too. This song was meant for one person in particular. Only person I cared to hear it."

Thome's stool rocked in the deepening water, a boat at low tide. B rested his hands on the table, like a pianist readying for a recital. His nails were green and black with dirt or decay.

Thome hacked and spat. Raw as his throat was, he hoped he had some reservoir of melody within him. He would play this song only once.

YEAR THREE

His fingers danced along the fretboard for the arpeggiated introduction. Like all his best works, it was in the minor key. Sorrow was always so much easier to mine than contentment. Across the table, B tapped along to the rhythm.

Thome contorted his fingers through jazz chords he'd accumulated like badges from musicians in every city. This one he'd learned from a pianist in Hell's Kitchen who overdosed a week later in a Harlem flophouse. The next was the sound of smoke obscuring recessed lights. The final chord of the intro was the sound of pink light on a young girl's braces.

Thome was supposed to open the first verse with a crooning "ooooooo," but his attempt to hit even that basic tone sent him into a coughing fit of such intensity that sticky blood webbed his strumming hand.

B continued his tapping as if the music hadn't stopped. Something under the surface of the water rubbed against Thome's ankle.

"I'm sorry," he said. He took a sip of coffee then tested his voice again, singing a simple scale in an octave that should have been no problem. His lungs disagreed. The world's moisture had finally flooded his bulkheads. The coughing nearly keeled him over.

At first, he thought B was reaching out in sympathy, like he meant to touch Thome but wasn't quite sure how to go about it. Instead, B was asking for the guitar.

"You play?" Thome could muster little more than a whisper.

B nodded.

"Some songs, once you start them, have to be finished—one way or another, I guess." He handed the guitar over.

B tested the strings, settled fingers into the same opening chord for Thome's secret song.

"Coming home," he said, like he'd just named the song himself.

What he played was undeniably Thome's piece. Those grey fingers found every chord at the required moment. But his playing, it evoked a melancholy Thome had never achieved.

At the verse, B's voice soared. It grew from the slow swirl of a protected bay to roiling surf colliding with a seaside cliff. Like ocean waves, the crest of his melody rode upon a buried half, the subliminal self.

The lyrics hardly seemed to be Thome's anymore. B sang of longing, of regret, of the imagined face of his loved one. He sang of an envisioned life, a home that could have been. The anger in the words was the buried half.

The seam at B's collar parted and opened downward. The slicker unfurled, taken by the winds of a hidden sea. Inside, there remained no body, only inky blackness. It was the secret, Thome knew, to B's unearthly euphony. Emptiness harboured the finest tonality. Music could not survive in a life fulfilled.

The water in the cabin turned to a maelstrom, swirling in time with B's frenetic fingers. Thick tentacles stretched from the torrents and wrapped themselves around Thome's body. They hauled him toward B. Every item in the cabin floated now, caught in subterranean eddies.

For Thome, there was only that all-encompassing blackness and its music. His music. The music he would play for his son. The accumulated sediment of sadness broken apart by that ocean of sound.

And the rain. Rain that, just now, had stopped.

Stopped for no reason at all.

Artificial Favouritism

by J.M. Faulkner

CEILING LIGHTS FLICKER. Our cutlery pauses over our plates.

The ship is dying, and so are we.

It's coughed out our last artificial meal for Dad and me; he calls it supper, so I guess it's *the Last Supper*.

"Don't be afraid of the dark, Stella."

He thinks I'm frightened because I'm twelve-nearly-thirteen, but I've given myself to fate.

Nicolai, the ship's AI, whispered that it favours my chances of rescue because of my age and the speed of intergalactic travel. Nicolai told me there's backup power for one freezer and grill, and it's identified one last source of meat.

Machinations

by Jen Mierisch

BACK THEN, MY job was to strip the corpses and bundle clothes for reuse. I tugged shoes and tossed them towards the heap.

On one shoe, a word was written, red dots against green: HELP. Our six-eyed Masters could not see colour.

Glancing around, I pried up the insole. The space held a key, an address, and a fervent request: deliver nitric acid to help build the weapon that would set us free.

Nowadays, I have all the sugar water I can drink, and a sunny apartment aboveground. The Masters may be ugly, but their rewards for loyalty are lovely.

A Space Pirate's Life

by Charlotte Langtree

THE SHIP WAS like nothing Jasper had seen before. Porous walls secreted a strange substance, and the floor throbbed beneath his feet. Leading his men into a small chamber, he stilled as a sharp hiss erupted.

Liquid flew from the wall onto his arm, searing clothes and skin.

"This ship's alive!"

He tried to run, but his boots stuck to the floor. With growing horror, he watched as his men were drenched in acidic ooze and devoured by the living ship they'd hoped to pilfer. When his turn came, death was a blessing.

Satisfied, the ship returned to its hibernation.

Sinlight Rising

by Kimberly Rei

SINLIGHT FLICKERED AROUND the planet below—a writhing, ancient welcome. It spiked in beautiful colours, beckoning us to visit. We'd been monitoring the activity for weeks, watching it grow. Two cycles ago, it began watching us. Now it was done watching. It was hunting.

I turned and ran down the corridor and around the corner, knowing nothing would save my body. Perhaps, I might be able to save the rest. Light exploded behind me. I leapt and felt a warm tendril grasp my ankle. With one desperate plea, I hurled my soul through an airless sliver of thought. To oblivion.

Prospector

by Rich Rurshell

BUZZING FILLED THE air as swarms of impregnators scoured the colony. The colonists were strewn around the settlement, paralysed, and riddled with eggs. Hosts to the next generation.

Sickly moonlight shone from the slick plating of the Prospector strolling through the chaos. It infiltrated the colony's information network, accessing files documenting the colony's eighty-seven-year history, before flying to the colony flagpole, incinerating the Fortuna Colony Flag with a pulse of energy, and constructing a beacon in its place.

Ascending to a vessel floating silently above the settlement, the Prospector left the swarms to prepare everything for the hatching.

Sunset

by Trevor Jess

I TOSS ANOTHER green log into the struggling fire. It sputters in protest. I'm only prolonging the inevitable.

The cold permeates my suit, licking away the little remnants of heat. I stare at the frozen lake.

It should be teeming with laughter, bodies splashing joyfully.

But it's barren.

Almost.

Beside me, a human block of ice. Crystallised. Their skin like fine salt.

They didn't last.

Neither will I.

I look skyward. Our once vibrant sun flickering in a death dance.

Not long now.

I sigh.

Will anyone wonder what happened to us?

A final ripple of light.

And I wait.

On the Edge of the Map

by Kaitlyn Arnett

IT'S SUPPOSED TO be a joke, marking the boundaries of space with a kraken next to the compass, or dragons curled alongside the edges of the page.

But the creature in front of them is real, solid, and there. It's every monster they tell stories about, all dagger-like fangs and sharp claws. Its body wraps around a star, and when it speaks, its voice is that of a thousand people.

"You have seen something not meant for human eyes," the voices call, "and you can stay no longer."

It moves, and when it stills, nothing remains.

Nothing, but the unknown.

Daddy Issues

by Sarina Dorie

I SAT ON the couch across from the psychiatrist. Dr Lonnie Perkins smiled patiently.

I cleared my throat. "I need your help. I have a monster addiction."

The older man adjusted his wire-rimmed glasses. "Lexi, what do you mean by monsters?"

I bit my lip.

"Are you saying you've been in abusive relationships?"

"Well, not like my mother. But that isn't what I mean. I want to stop my obsession with ghosts, werewolves, and zombies." And every other sexy beast that went bump in the night.

His weathered brow crinkled even more. "You mean imaginary monsters?"

"They're real."

"Oh, I see." He scribbled something on his notepad. Already I could tell this wasn't going well.

"Let's go back to something you said a moment ago. What were your mother's relationships like while you were growing up?"

I sighed in frustration. "Okay, I get it. They were monsters, but figuratively, not literally." I thought back to my mom's many boyfriends. "My first memory is of 'Uncle' Marty giving me this." I rolled up my sleeve and showed off my cigarette burn scar. "My mom didn't believe me, but when she saw him do it to the dog, she finally broke up with him."

"That must have been hard for a child."

Tears filled my eyes. That hadn't been the worst of it. "She told me my dad was a monster. Not a mythological monster or anything sexy—just a human devoid of emotions. He'd stolen her life-savings and left while she was pregnant with me."

He pushed the box of tissues closer. His smile was kind and I felt at ease, which was odd since I usually had a hard time feeling comfortable around men—human men.

I took a tissue and dabbed at my eyes. "After Uncle Marty, there were others. 'Uncle Benny' used to beat my older brother. Jimmy was two years older than me. He was always trying to protect me and would yell for me to go lock myself in the bathroom when Uncle Benny was in one of his drunken rages." I could see Benny's squat, red face. It was hard to imagine why my mother had called him handsome.

Lonnie nodded. "I can see why you believe in monsters."

I had a sinking suspicion he didn't understand. "When I was scared and ran into the woods behind the trailer park, there was a ghost I met out there. He was kind and talked to me when I was afraid—afraid of Mama's boyfriends, I mean." Aside from being pale and devoid of colour, Bo looked normal. He dressed in a T-shirt and jeans, and had a friendly, honest face. He hadn't been scary.

"What did he say?"

"Nice things. Bo told me it wasn't my fault, even when Mama said it was. He only talked about happy things and avoided questions about how he died. But sometimes I got little pieces out of him: the year he died—the same year I was born; how he'd been going to night school so he could get a better job, so he was hardly ever home to see what his wife had been up to; and that his wife had killed him when he flushed her drugs down the toilet and threatened to take their son away if she didn't clean up her act." I'd been young the first time I'd met him. By the time I was nine, I had guessed that the dark line above his collar had been where someone had slit his throat.

"Bo said he wanted to help me. He wanted me to have a safe place to go when it got to be too much. But he couldn't leave the woods. That was his 'territory' because that's where his wife had buried his body." I swallowed the lump in my throat. "If he tried to leave, he would fade away and no longer exist."

The psychiatrist chewed on his pencil.

"One night, when Uncle Benny was high, he went all psycho and tore the phone out of the wall. My mom had overdosed again and was having a seizure, but Uncle Benny didn't want us to get the police involved because of his record. He grabbed my brother by the hair and punched him in the face. I was so scared, I didn't know what to do. I tried to jump on Uncle Benny's back to get him off my brother, but he threw me off and I broke my wrist. I ran to the neighbours, but the old lady who lived next door told me to go away. I tried two more doors and asked them to call the police. Then I saw Jimmy's face pressed up to the window, unconscious and bleeding.

"I didn't know what to do, so I called for Bo's help. He watched me from the edge of the woods, his expression sad. I knew he couldn't do anything. He'd always told me he couldn't enter the trailer park." I stifled a sob.

"It sounds like you felt powerless," the psychiatrist said.

I nodded. "The thing is, Bo did leave the woods. He floated into the trailer and, in a burst of energy, hurled the television onto Uncle Benny's head. He turned to me and smiled one last time. Then he faded away. He'd used up all his energy, and he disappeared. He sacrificed himself for Jimmy and me.

"An ambulance eventually came, but it was too late for my mom. It was only after the police came and tore up the trailer searching for evidence of who had killed Benny that I found the photograph of Bo. He was young and handsome and holding a two-year-old boy. He stood with his arm around my pregnant mother." I broke into sobs.

Lonnie waited until I was done crying. The eraser to his

pencil was gone and the metal now mangled where he had chewed it. "Have you considered you might have seen the photograph prior to that night, and your subconscious invented this ghost to cope with the violence in your life?"

"It wasn't my imagination. Bo—my dad—was real. Monsters are real, and they're just like my father. They're kind and strong and better than human men in every way. But they always have to leave. And some of them... I want them to love me so bad, but I just drive them away."

"It sounds like you want a powerful monster; the more dangerous the better, so he can protect you."

I nodded. For a heartbeat, I thought he understood me.

He went on. "You don't want someone normal, someone human, because no man can live up to the fantasy of your father."

"Stop saying that. It's not a fantasy. I'm not crazy."

"No, of course not. Oh, look at the clock. Our forty-five minutes are up. We can explore this further next week."

I snorted. Like I was planning on coming back.

I left in such a huff, I only remembered my umbrella once I was outside in the twilight and saw it was raining. The door of the cement building locked behind me, and Lonnie didn't answer when I called from my cell. Circling the building to see if there was a backdoor, I spotted Lonnie through a sliver of curtains. I raised my hand, about to tap at the window, but stopped.

Lonnie reached behind his head and unzipped his hair

and skin like it was a jacket. His sweater parted, revealing darkness. The translucent shadow stepped out of his human clothes and flesh. My eyes widened. I had no idea what he was, but my pulse raced with longing.

Maybe I would go back after all.

Weak Flesh

by Maggie D. Brace

SNAKING IN SILENTLY, the cord slowly entwined my ankle, producing a sharp electric jolt as it reached my calf. Intent on disabling the mainframe, I kicked at it with my free foot, then ignored it as best I could. It advanced sinuously up my thigh, then my torso.

Batting at it absentmindedly, it encircled my wrist, then inserted its pronged end into my ear canal. At once a crackling static sound enveloped my brain, while my body became paralyzed. A whining metallic voice menacingly pulsed through my body, "Your weak flesh will now feed our matrix, cease your struggling!"

Torched

by J.W. Garrett

THROUGH THE MISTS of the gloaming, Elspeth came to, slick with sweat, her arms and legs bound to the stake. She blinked, focusing on the members of the tiny town in Maine where she'd been just passing through. A small number of them had gathered. Now they watched her, their eyes eager. Hungry.

Blending in had been easy. Becoming faceless, a nobody, it was what she did. That was the life she led. Three days ago, thinking back, that had been when she'd healed the young girl, with herbs she'd found in the forest and a spell or two. The little thing had been out of her mind with fever. She'd return to full health soon. The local doctor had given up the little girl for dead. Bed rest and leaches he'd prescribed. Elspeth scoffed. Was she supposed to let the child die because of the ignorant town's people? Yet, now that the child had come through the worst of it, word apparently had spread. Humans—they weren't worth the oxygen they consumed.

"Look," a gruff voice called out, "the sorcerer still lives." Her gaze shot to the man. A sneer twisted his lips when he chuckled. "But not for long. We'll protect our community, our loved ones from her kind."

The man's eyes gleamed behind dark pools of heated pleasure as he spat at her feet and lit the pyre, announcing, "Time for the show." He leaned in closer. "I'll watch you dance. Burn, witch, burn."

Her eyes slammed shut, lips peeled back, Elspeth murmured the incantation. And as the wind bent to her will, the band of men hushed and stilled. Struck dumb, their faces laced with fear, they watched the slow crawl of fire licking at her feet reach outward to encompass them. As Elspeth summoned greater gusts of air, the dancing flames found each man. Their belated attempts at flight useless, the men's terror washed back through her, the tall fingers of fire soon silencing their crying pleas.

The air popped and crackled, spitting smoke from the smouldering flesh among the piles of simmering ash. Energy depleted, Elspeth sagged against the stake. Movement shifted among the undergrowth, catching her attention. Behind her, Elspeth felt multiple hands working the knots at her arms and feet. Minutes later, she collapsed on the ground with a groan, grateful for the earth and foliage once again beneath her fingers. Breathing in her lifeblood, she raised her gaze to those who'd dared to release her. Staggering to a stand, a small circle surrounded her, their eyes wide—the family whose child she'd healed.

Her feet blistered with burns and covered in filth and sweat, she nodded her thanks then slowly picked her way

free. Lifting her soot covered face to the rising moon, Elspeth called forth lightning, thunder, and rain, and clearing a path through the stench of burning bodies and death penetrating the air, she plodded forward.

The embers and ruined flesh sighed and hissed as they cooled. Behind her, the scene of carnage faded into nothingness. Ahead, the wind moaned and whined, inviting her into the darkness. Elspeth let it take her. She seethed.

The town wouldn't soon forget her name.

Future Shock

by Steven Holding

THE SYNTHETIC ASSASSIN slipped through a rip in time, arriving on my side, armed and accompanied. Recognising his comrade, I gasped.

It was me. Thirty years older.

As the impossible pair approached, the artificial gunslinger singled me out: an electronic hitman holding me frozen in his sights.

Suddenly, I was pointing at myself.

"KILL HIM!!!!"

The bright blaze of the pulsing laser rifle knocked me off my feet.

Feeling my life-force slip away, I gazed up towards my future.

"Why?"

"To spare you the pain of what's to come," the old me whispered as we both winked out of existence.

Judgement

by Chris Bannor

I DID EVERYTHING by the book, followed every rule and regulation. None of that matters now.

I can see inside the window, and nothing changes the judgement they passed. I want to scream that I did what I had to so we could survive.

The ship gets further away as they continue to watch.

I try to keep my face still, but terror eats away at me, and pain is etched in my bones. I turn my head and my body rotates. Now there is no one to see my last moments.

There's no witness in the void of space.

It's Out There

by Constantine E. Kiousis

DAVID COWERED IN a dark corner of his bedroom, eyes wet behind fractured glasses, body shaking, arms clasped around folded legs. He could hear it walking down the hallway, heavy footsteps thudding towards the locked door.

He'd spent his whole life searching for them, dedicated every waking moment on deciphering clues others dismissed as conspiracy theory fuel. But he'd figured it out: the cattle mutilations, the crop circles, the sightings, the abductions.

He'd pieced it together.

He'd discovered the truth.

What never crossed his mind was that he wasn't supposed to.

The door exploded.

David screamed.

They'd come for him.

A Father's Love

by Reuben Paul

THE MUSIC PLAYED, soft and romantic, throughout the burrow and they danced slowly to the tune.

With her head on his shoulder, and her ears draped down his back, he led the sway, recalling how he'd wooed her back in their younger days, before all the responsibility that family brought. How they'd frolicked in the fields chasing butterflies and enjoying the morning sun.

Their beautiful leverets, the spoils of their love, bounced excitedly around them and he smiled, lips curling to reveal white fangs.

He'd forever mourn her death, but at least the babies would have a hearty meal tonight.

Garden Guardian

by Maggie D. Brace

ROBERT HAD BEEN putting off tackling the gloomy old dead tree for months now. It drooped forlornly on the outskirts of his yard, giving off definite neglected garden vibes. He resigned himself to a morning of uncomfortable physical labour, followed by a festive garden party with friends later.

He began chopping half-heartedly, but as each swing was met with a satisfyingly resounding *thunk*, he began to enjoy himself. He got into a rhythm and paused only when he needed to take a breather.

At first, he thought the movements he glimpsed out of the corner of his eye were scuttling leaves, but every time he stopped his swing to look, it was gone.

He continued with his work, enjoying the crisp weather and the exertion of his pent-up energy.

There it is again! He frowned as the small, dark, shadowy streak blurred past him again, the hair on his neck raising uncomfortably. It flitted just beyond his vision and then disappeared.

He moved toward the motion with the axe draped over his shoulder. Suddenly, the small furry creature shot out from the underbrush and latched its razor-sharp teeth onto his shin. He howled in surprise and pain and began shaking his leg to fling it off. It didn't budge. He gingerly reached down and tried to pry its jaws apart. Still no effect.

He began to feel light-headed—perhaps this woodland beast had pumped some sort of toxin into him. He reeled woozily.

He knew what he needed to do. Taking careful aim with his axe, he struck the shadowy menace right below its scrawny neck. Its body limply dropped to the ground, but the teeth remained imbedded in his ankle bone. Looking around in desperation for any assistance, he realised he only had so much time left before he passed out.

Resigning himself, he hacked into his leg just above the tenaciously clinging fiend, before slowly lapsing into unconsciousness.

***

Upon waking, he found himself surrounded by the concerned faces of his party guests. George was kneeling down, bandaging his leg. Robert shrieked and tried to warn them about the hideous monster that had attacked him, pointing to where its crumpled body lay.

His friends exchanged concerned looks over his head, and he realised there was no crumpled creature body, no gluttonous monstrosity attached to his leg. No signs of *any* struggle, save a missed swing of the axe.

He decided to keep his mouth shut about his run in with the wilding for the time being.

YEAR THREE

As his friends carefully assisted him back inside, he swore he heard a derisively mocking chatter emanating from the dead tree.

Happiness is a Warm Android

by John H. Dromey

LEO WAS A recurrent victim of the race to put a man on Mars.

After each catastrophic failure, the test pilot was reassembled in a higgledy-piggledy fashion until he had very few remaining original parts. He was more machine than man.

Whether bulked up until he could barely fit into a spacesuit, or when crushed nearly flat by the collapsing hull of an experimental rocket, his girlfriend Gemma stuck with him through thick and thin.

"What attracts you to Leo?" a reporter asked Gemma.

"I don't know about his artificial heart, but his *hard drive* is in the right place."

Nightmares

by Keith R. Burdon

THE ONCE BRIGHT wallpaper pattern is now a ghost of its former self. In places it's peeling off the wall, patches of black mould playing a grim version of hide and seek.

A single bed occupies one corner. She makes sure she keeps it away from the wall. In her nightmares the mould makes its way inexorably down the surface, on to the duvet and, finally, terrifyingly, onto her skin. A deathly tattoo. Unconsciously, she scratches at her arms.

Soon, she hears those familiar heavy footsteps on the stairs. In this forgotten room the monster doesn't live under the bed.

Memories of Murder

by Archit Joshi

*T*HE DOORBELL RANG. *Kwan, palm slick with sweat, grasped the door handle and paused. The arrival was expected, but unwelcome.*

***

Number #1808 paced his room. His configurations bobbed around him, a hologram keeping up with his manic steps. The System Reset menu was open. One click would make him vanish.

Master Kwan would be furious. He was used to reprimands for adding salt to the coffee or messing up Master Kwan's mood playlists. But this time, it was serious. Master Kwan was in for a world of hurt. And in possible danger.

***

A trembling middle-aged woman... A musty, dark room, curtains drawn... Shards of a broken vase. The rancid smell of blood. Cicadas chirping, a shovel thumping...

Kwan jerked up from his memory reinstall and yanked the wires attached to his temples. These weren't his memories. But he vaguely recognised the flashes; the room was similar to a murder report he'd watched months ago.

A bedside computer beeped with an error screen: *Installation Interrupted!*

Kwan cursed Number #1808. The idiot must've corrupted his memory. Kwan was convinced his AI was just an 'A', but lacked the 'I'.

"They're evolving, Kwan Ssi," the customer reps kept repeating. "Wait for the version rollouts."

On extracting your memories onto a microchip, your AI was supposed to sort them, archive negative experiences so they didn't cause troubled dreams, and delete irrelevant junk. AI's solution for an unburdened, relaxing sleep.

But AIs were supposed to be careful to separate Personal Experiences from Consumed Content. The fool had turned his past recollection of the news report into a theatrical personal experience.

He glanced at the neighbouring bed to see if they were experiencing similar problems. It was vacant. Before he could go looking, another beep from his computer arrested his attention.

Kwan reattached the wires to his temples and initiated a restore. The computer revived his memories from a previous backup and slid out a retractable slot fitted with a memory microchip, engraved with the owner's name.

Kwan read the name and froze. Number #1808 hadn't corrupted his memory, he'd swapped it.

Hyun-Wu unwillingly appeared for his morning assessment, a ghost in a skin. Number #7555 sprayed him with inspection rays. Moments later, a holographic status chart appeared.

The sleep quotient was critically low. Hyun-Wu reached out and maximised the sleep slider, feeling his energy rising in tandem.

"Don't you have one for minimising regret?" he grumbled.

"I do not have a setting for minimising regret, Master Hyun-Wu."

Hyun-Wu had already shuffled into the kitchen. AIs were not quite experts of rhetoric. If the government hadn't mandated AIs in every home, Number #7555 would've been in a dumpster.

"Regret is a neurological response. I can only reconfigure physiological imbalances."

Hyun-Wu slumped into a chair, a piece of heavily buttered toast on his plate.

He found feeble delight in remembering games of catch, sunny park picnics, road trips, and movie nights. Remembering oneself through another's eyes was surely a treat. He appeared smiling, cheerful, and loving. Hyun-Wu wondered whether his own memories of the same incidents were so pure.

There were also glimpses of kisses stolen in a college bathroom, of heartache, of longing, and belonging. But these memories Hyun-Wu left alone. He respected his son's privacy enough.

Brushing crumbs off his shirt, he prepared himself mentally. The thought of the difficult conversation he needed to have with Kwan filled every nerve-ending in his body with dread.

"Have a great day, Master Hyun-Wu," the AI greeted as he was heading out.

"Screw yourself, you shiny red bastard."

"I do not have the necessary biology, Master Hyun-Wu."

Hyun-Wu was already out the door.

**

I'm coming over.

The text had tormented Kwan. This could go a million ways, but each ended with Kwan sending his father to jail.

He kept replaying snippets of the alien memory he'd reinstalled despite himself.

"He deserves the truth!"

"He CANNOT know. That night was a mistake…a weak moment… Just forget it happened, move on."

"He's my son, dammit."

"He's my son, too. And you agreed my wife and I would bring him up, and you would leave us alone. If she finds out—"

"I don't care if your wife finds out. I want to see him." The woman produced a brown parcel. *"Or I'll be forced to*

go public."

The next part troubled Kwan the most. Not the underhanded blackmail, or the ensuing ferocious quarrel, or even the murder. Kwan's father had calculatingly scanned the room, evaluating his options. Like a cold-blooded killer.

After hours chewing these memories, Kwan had convinced himself they could only cause more pain. He'd restored his own backup and was about to crush his father's microchip when the text arrived.

A similar message had come yesterday but things had been wildly different. A pleasant day together, an overnight stay, a hearty breakfast, and a friendly goodbye. A happy memory in the making.

But Hyun-Wu had fled in the night, and instead of pancakes, a thousand knots filled Kwan's stomach.

An hour later, the doorbell rang. Kwan, palm slick with sweat, grasped the door handle and paused. He prayed for the courage to face the man who'd not only deceived him his entire life, but had sunk to despicable levels to cover his tracks.

He finally opened the door. A defeated man stood outside. His father's eyes were beseeching, his face contorted. His arm was folded behind his back.

"Give me a chance to explain, son?" He made to move his arm when a blast of warm air whizzed past Kwan's ear.

"Oh, no you don't, you evil murderer!"

Kwan turned. Number #1808 stood behind him, an

N654 Neutrino handgun poised. Kwan turned back again. The charge had passed clean through his father's chest. Hyun-Wu collapsed, agonised surprise plastered on his face.

"He must've had a gun, Master Kwan! But he can't hurt you anymore." Number #1808 thundered to the door to inspect the fallen man. He'd saved Master Kwan's life.

Kwan stood paralysed. Number #1808 pulled out Hyun-Wu's twisted arm from underneath his body. And then stumbled backwards with a shriek. In the dying clutch of Kwan's father was a bouquet.

The hyacinths, originally purple, were turning a dark crimson.

The Necromancer's Sin

by Bernardo Villela

LADISLAV MOURNED LONG. Whilst it was true the black death had killed his family, some felt the length and depth of his mourning unseemly. He knew deaths were not something one overcame fast; this is what drew him to necromancy.

He refined his skills after work and before meals with animals large and small. Then graduated but failed with his father, brothers, and sisters. His study of his mother's necrotising corpse began in the summer of his thirteenth year.

No one knew his mother was with him still. The plague doctor had come to dispose of her body, but Ladislav told the beak-masked man he'd already taken care of her remains and sent him on his way with whatever coin he had handy.

He lived alone and unbothered, in his perverse interpretation of peace, in the miasmic environs of his home. The last of his line, he expected the black death to take him as well, but it did not, even though his mother festered in the house. He took this to mean he owed a penance for some forgotten sin.

As repentance, Ladislav did what could to keep himself working and fed. He used the family's stores of coin, sold goods, and worked as a labourer in various trades as his parents had.

He was well-liked, though people found him too dour. They knew something was not quite right about him. He smelled odd, rambled about seeking forgiveness, and was pitied.

Now old and nearly unable to work, his analysis of his mother's cadaver was complete at long last. God's grace had allowed him to witness the decomposition of his mother and learn where he'd erred in the past. He was too young and inexperienced. Necromancy takes a lifetime to master, but now in his eighties—the eldest in the village, by a score—he was ready.

Checking over his texts, preparing for the ancient rite, it was as if he looked at his mother for the first time in years. He'd tended to her as best as he could. Cleaned up her postmortem defecation, rinsed her in oils. The stench, however, could never be quelled. He tried preserving her in salt, but the bloat set in and had never truly left. Attempts to preserve her were defeated by the passage of time. There was no peak he could scale to pack her in ice, so the decay was not arrested. Shuttered windows concealed the flies from the world outside until their death. The salts slowed the liquefaction of her soft tissue, but at this point she had no eyes, and her throat was puffed.

Though he no longer wanted to do it, he began the rite.

His magics worked. She creaked, lifting her crumbling

carcass into a sitting position, caked salts and unctions sliding off her decayed corpse. Her voice was stifled, but he could hear her speak.

"Ladislav, you dolt, is there a cure for the black death?"

He froze, staring at her desiccated, discoloured face.

"Can you re-form my eyes and make me see? Open my throat and make me speak clearly? Raise up your father, brothers, sisters who you separated me from? Was bringing me back in this state worth it? Look at you, my boy—a decrepit, defeated old man who threw his life away in this house, and for what? To raise the monster you once called Mother? To squander the gift you'd been given when you avoided the Reaper?"

He cried and dropped his grimoire. When his eyes cleared, he saw his mother lying on her back as she had been. He hadn't performed the ritual, but, instead, had witnessed its probable outcome.

He realised the sin he was being punished for was not in the distant past, but one that had continued over the course of decades as he wasted his life.

He clutched his chest and fell to the ground. The plague might not have killed him, but it had robbed him of his life just the same, as he locked himself away to play God.

In silence, he begged his Saviour's forgiveness until his heart stopped and his life ceased.

YEAR THREE

Garrote Vil

by Maggie D. Brace

WITH THE WIND gently rustling past and the dappled shade from the foliage, the 100 degree weather was almost bearable. Tubing down the river was the ideal excursion to beat the heat. The cool water lapped around us, almost too chilly, despite the air temperature. Jordy had a small inner tube for a cooler of beer and the variety of plants and animals we floated by was astonishing. Avoiding a few fallen trunks and protruding rocks was easy enough, and interspersed with several roiling rapids, the lazy current kept us moving smoothly back toward the car. Approaching the last rapid, all seemed right with the world, until Jordy's scream broke the silence. As I came abreast of his tube, I was at first confused. His head was slightly askew on his neck. Then it unceremoniously toppled into the water. As I opened my mouth to scream, the taut wire stretching across the river bit into my neck as well.

Annihilation

by Victor Nandi

BLOOD SPATTERED AS bullets tore through soft flesh. Olivia and her followers fell. Their bodies lay still for a moment. Then, electric sparks sizzled from their artificial limbs that yanked them to their feet.

Olivia rose, stabbed her metallic hand into a guard's chest, and walked into the control room. Teary-eyed, she hit some buttons.

"Target cities locked," the console said.

A slot lit up displaying: *Insert key to launch warhead.*

"You need the key." A dying guard grinned.

Relief filled Olivia's face. But it soon changed to helpless horror as metallic nanoparticles extended from her fingertip forming a key.

The Rift

by Bernardo Villela

ALL ABOARD WERE awestruck. Creating the dimensional rift was simple, but from it came a spacecraft identical to ours.

The mission commander's words echoed in my mind: *Conducting geopolitical and scientific experiments over there shields us from consequence.*

"Full speed ahead!" I said.

Our comms buzzed.

"This is the *Nautilus*." From our twin ship I hear my voice speaking. It was us from another dimension.

"Thanks, our tech failed."

My heart rate tripled. We looked at one another.

"Houston!"

"Remember your objective."

We proceeded. The rift closed behind us sealing our doppelgänger's fate. We were expendable, all versions of us.

Abraham

by Patrick Winters

I WOULD'VE DIED alongside the other colonists aboard the *Abraham*, if they hadn't pulled me from the crash site.

Twisted and strange, but not completely inhuman. They patched my wounds. Hooked me up to machines that kept me paralysed. Started using me. Stimulating me, to my disgust. Extracting and collecting what they needed.

Years passed and they started to change. Their young came to view me as the process continued, their features softer, paler—familiar, somehow.

Made me feel like some animal in a zoo. But then I realised the reverence in their eyes.

Like a child, before a father.

The Migration

by N.E. Rule

WHERE THERE WAS an ocean, there are now craters to rival the moon.

Animal skeletons of every ilk litter around me like a Noah's Ark disaster documentary. With limited space per transit, many species demised on this waystation.

Despite my hazmat suit, I draw in a breath, imagining it's the once brisk air of the surrounding Arctic Circle. Our scientists say after the prescribed cleanse, we may return. But not in my lifetime. Sweat trickling down my spine reminds me the day will soon turn deadly hot. I drive the final detonator into the crumbling earth before boarding the airship.

Small Print

by Simon Clarke

GERRY WAS ASLEEP. His left eyeball pulsed and popped itself out of its socket and slithered onto the floor, heading for the door. It slithered along the hallway and out through the cat flap. Cybertronic Systems organs had state of the art neuro-connect functionality hence the searing pain in Gerry's head, causing him to scream and tear at his face in agony. Outside, his cat licked aqueous humour from its paws and padded off satisfied, tail flicking the air.

When they said there were sometimes rejection issues, Gerry assumed he might be doing the rejecting, not the other way round.

Where Stalks Grow

by A.H. Syme

SHE LOVED HIM. It was clear in the way she stroked his face and whispered in his ears until love echoed around her.

Her heart burned to touch deeper, but it couldn't be. So, she showed her love by trying to wash the blood from his feet, a drop in the vast ocean of blood that stained him. She pretended it was syrup, but sometimes there were clumps of hair.

Hers, a clandestine love; hidden from her thieving son.

He must never know, not after the beating she had given him over a handful of beans for an old cow.

Eye of the Storm Giant

by Shawn M. Klimek

THE AMERICAN LIFTED his snow-covered goggles onto his forehead, revealing an eyepatch beside one good eye. He gave the lead rope two short pulls before shouting angrily into the wind, "Norbu!"

His mountain-guide's wizened face turned back to squint inquisitively through the blizzard. "Yes, sir?"

"How much higher until we see the giant?" he griped.

"The giant is mostly underground," Norbu reminded him, regretting their agreement. "But look up there. He pointed to a snow-covered outcropping. "That's the tip of his nose."

"Just lead me to his giant eye," demanded the American, revealing a gun. "I came for his eye."

Bad Boy!

by Maggie D. Brace

THE SLURPING SOUND grew louder and louder, accompanied by increasingly more alarming growling. "Knock it off, Boxy! Stop licking the carpet!" Jared called out from his bed, rolling over and pulling a pillow over his head.

He had pulled an extra shift last night and wasn't in the mood to be disturbed by the damn dog this early in the morning.

The noise became so annoying he pulled himself out of bed, scratching himself through his droopy boxers.

Eyes half shut, he stepped out into the hallway, tripping over the now skinless remains of his new roomie. "Boxy, not again!"

The Cat and Me

by A.H. Syme

THE CAT JUMPED from the dresser to the floor in a smooth, effortless motion, and as it moved, it appeared like black liquid gloss had morphed into the form of a feline. It was a small cat, thin, with large green eyes that gleamed in the moon's wane light. Eyes that caught the moonbeams, reflecting them and making them glow as if its soul had surfaced in its eyeshine—supernatural, mysterious, eerie and sinister.

I watched it move—gentle and soft—across the floorboards, in strides as silent as snowfall, its coat shimmering in the trapped moonlight captured within the windowpane. The cat approached its mistress and nudged and rubbed its forehead against her cheek, but she remained still. It rubbed again, up and down, the soft folds of pale skin creasing upwards and then settling back on the woman's cheek to its original flat plane. It seemed to press its nose and then its mouth against the corner of her lips, but from the angle I sat, and in the gloom, I couldn't be sure. It looked to hold this position for a long time, only the occasional flick of its tail bringing movement to the scene's stillness, breaking the surreal image of a Machiavellian painting.

It broke away and padded across to me, soundless, staring, holding me in its enormous gaze. I wanted to kill it, but I was exhausted from struggling with its mistress, so I sat, my breath easing from its panting, my heart trying to find its usual sluggish pace.

An old man doing a young man's tastes.

It stopped near my feet and then moved between my legs, wandering somewhere under the table, then re-emerged by my left leg. I thought of kicking it, but my heart said no, and my lungs said breathe, both unanimous in their warning plea of saving their unhealthy abode. So, I watched the cat pad away and leave through the open kitchen door like an apparition, but it's a ghost that leaves crimson paw prints of blood in its passing, and where it treads in some spilt sugar, turns the white crystals to a soft, delicate pink.

***

A few hours after I returned home, Senior Detective Constable Andrews arrived. He now sits with a coffee cup in his hand, his female junior by rank and years writing notes in a flip pad.

"As I said, Mr Sloane, we are interviewing all the neighbours to glean any bit of information we can. Everything is helpful in a homicide. You never know what can turn into vital evidence."

He smiled at me, but it didn't reach his sharp, brown eyes that sat deep on either side of his proud, eagle-shaped nose. Both, giving his face the same powerful countenance of a bird of prey, a raptor that missed nothing, as his eyes seemed to scour every part of me.

"I have lived next door to Julia for ten years, and in all my time, there has never been any…." I floundered, looking for the right word. "Any disturbances," I said.

"No comings and goings of gentleman callers?" Andrews asked.

"None, Julia wasn't like that," I said.

"Like what?" Andrews asked, raising his eyebrows to stress his question.

"Like what you are implying," I said, my tone brisk. I took a sip of my tea to calm myself. *Steady, now. Steady.*

Andrews continued. "It seems the other neighbours concur. She apparently didn't have friends in and out and didn't have strangers to her door, and if she did, she definitely didn't invite them in. They say she kept her house tightly locked," Andrews said.

"Yes, she did. She was a sensible young woman," I said, slurping my tea. It was allowed. Men approaching old age could get away with such things, and although I could feel gas moving like swollen waves of pain in my belly, caused by the tension I felt, I didn't think farting would be so nicely excused by society—not yet.

Andrews shifted his position in the seat, crossed his other leg and sipped his coffee.

"What happened to her?" I asked, putting down my cup. The china clattered against the coffee table as my hand trembled slightly.

"Are you all right?" Andrews asked, his voice smooth like silk; spiders' silk.

No. No, I'm not, and you bloody well know it. If I had my knife, I would carve your ugly nose off your face, plunge and plunge it into your skin, puncturing flesh, muscle, till I hit bone, as I did with that girl. And I would gouge your beady eyes out with a spoon.

I stopped. Coming to the sudden awareness that my fingers that clasped the teaspoon were twisting it fiercely in the air as if trying to hollow it out.

Andrews smiled that insincere smile.

"It looked like she had been getting some sugar for someone. There is a bag on her table. A kitchen cupboard slightly opened. You wouldn't do that for a stranger, would you?" Andrews asked, tilting his head at me.

"Of course not; she must have known the killer," I said.

"Oh, she did," Andrews said. "She knew him as a nice, older gentleman who lived next door." He put down his coffee cup and stood.

"Come along, Mr Sloane. The cat's out of the bag, so to speak." He glanced down at the bottom of my trousers. My eyes followed suit, but I could see nothing.

"Turn them around," he said.

I did. There, on the back cuff, a red, bright paw print.

***

Death row gives you a lot of time to sit and

contemplate. I was to receive a lethal injection in two days' time, after waiting eight years for it to come. Many nights I tossed and turned, not from fear of death, not for my soul's plight; the devil could have me. We might end up mates.

No. I tossed and turned, wishing I had skinned that cat alive and nailed it to the wall, but that wasn't the real cause of my restlessness, of what confounded me the most. It was a thought that had crept into my mind a few years back, an idea that so annoys me; it nags my mind, bringing me unrest, one that always comes as sure as my stale breath.

That cat, that night, as it had crept to its mistress and pressed its nose to her lips, that cat, I'm sure—almost sure—had kissed her; kissed her gently, long, slow and sweet. Hadn't it? Perhaps. I'm almost positive it had. Like a lover's final kiss goodbye. A deliberate, calculated move like that friggin' condemning mark it left on me. I shake my head, but the scene remains; I toss and turn—that damn, infernal cat.

But one thing I'm certain of—and I don't doubt because I have nothing to care about, not here amongst the living—when they take me down the hall and strap me to the bed and stick the needle in, I'm going to fart. I'm going to let it rip, and I hope to hell, I shit my pants.

Leader of the Pack

by Charlotte Langtree

THE WOMAN WALKED alone.

"She'll have food tokens," Jenna said.

Five men nodded. Jenna fingered the trigger of the holo-knife she'd stolen from a rival; it fooled scans and would leave a pretty hole.

They cornered the woman at a junction, weapons raised. Golden eyes flickered. Jenna's gut clenched. It was a droid mole: a trap to catch rebels.

It opened its mouth. Scorching flames shot out, burning Jenna's men to a crisp. Jenna screamed. The flames were hot, but the burn of the dragon-droid's laser planting a chip in her heart was worse.

She bowed. "What is your command?"

News from Sister No 1

by Joel R. Hunt

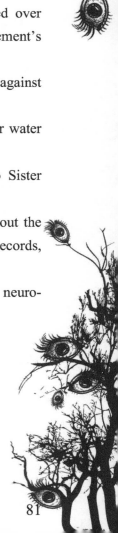

G ARZO GRABBED MY shoulder.

"Quick, check the prime stream."

I tuned in. The newscast flickered over my vision, showing our movement's spokesperson, Sister No1, smiling.

"Glorious day!" she said. "Our struggle against Pleasure Inc is finally over!"

I frowned. Didn't the megacorp still control our water supply and the air farms?

Then the CEO of Pleasure Inc stepped up to Sister No1's side.

"This morning," he said, "Pleasure Inc bought out the Anarcho-Libertarian Collective, including its records, assets…"

He held out a trigger, thumb at the ready. My neuro-implants began to itch.

"…and the life support codes of its operatives."

Cool Kids

by S. Jade Path

REN STOOD ON the gore-slicked dancefloor, blood sluicing down her armour. Dancing holograms still gyrating in the wet smears, and the pounding music seemingly quiet in the absence of screams.

Staring, smiling, at what remained of the Syndicate Children—the Cool Kids.

They had made me. Saved me. She sneered at that thought. They had taken her dead, junkie's body, fused armour-scale tech to it, trained it to kill.

Made her into this abomination.

***

Ren sat on a ledge, 172 floors above the street, combat boots swinging.

Whispering, "Cool Kids never sleep."

Leaning forwards, she pushed off, falling—finally—to sleep.

Cheap-Ass

by Rich Rurshell

DANA TORE THROUGH the Obsidian Plaza Hotel, despatching security with ease. Her body had cost a pretty penny, but her speed, reflexes, and combat capabilities were unrivalled. All four limbs and her torso had been replaced with top-of-the-line Linneman Industries augmentations. It was ironic she was on her way to assassinate their president, Charles Linneman.

Dana burst into the penthouse suite to find Linneman and his entourage eating dinner.

"Nice augs," said Linneman. "Shame you didn't buy our firewalls, too."

Linneman manipulated a holographic interface in his palm, and Dana began dancing.

"Tonight's entertainment, gentlemen!" he cried.

Inclusion

by N.E. Rule

MY STOMACH GROWLS in anticipation of the U8-rations downloading to my dwellment dispenser on sign-on.

I push down memories of Mom's last warning during her D-leet ceremony: Don't accept it. But living as a grid-free hacker during the Great Overpopulation is a struggle.

Employment is impossible without it. Convertors say it opens doors, literally. Also, GloBank downloads cash creds to your braindrive directly.

The SysCtrl swipes at the bloodtear after the microchip's implanted. He smiles reassuringly as LiFi starts up. The eye-con app for D-leet registers 9125. Now that I'm assimilated to the system, I've ten years to break it.

Roots

by Colleen Anderson

THE LAYERING OF nanobytes into his hypodermis laced Nirved's nerves with lava. The pain muffled him. The nanotechnologist paused.

"No," Nirved grunted. "Continue."

The protective barrier had been set. Planting came next.

Large swaths of jungle lay barren, plants crisping under the sun's inferno. Trees toppled throughout countries, and oxygen thinned. People died with the trees.

At best, this experiment could save the world. At worst, Nirved would die before Earth did.

With Great Power

by Darlene Holt

WHEN CYDOCS BECAME a thing, they needed volunteers to test out the new ware. I was among the first, opting for a cybernetic arm which promised never-before-seen strength.

I won arm wrestling contests with ease, effortlessly ripped doors from hinges, and threw blows like a sledgehammer with my fist.

One night, I challenged a stranger with neuralware processors to a fight. He hacked the arm before I could even swing. It turned on me, titanium fingers clutching my throat, constricting with every attempted breath. The stranger's laughter lingered as the metal hand tightened, my human arm powerless to stop it.

Danse Macabre

by Joshua D. Taylor

MAX LOOKED AROUND the room that was covered in Jennifer's splattered remains. He had no idea what happened. One minute he was trying out the new salsa dancing skills he had downloaded. The next thing he knew he was covered in gore.

A notification from the developer popped up in his vision: *You may have received the incorrect skills with your recent purchase. Your account has been refunded.*

Max scrolled through the list of new skills in the salsa dance program and saw one titled "Dismember."

He looked around at the mess and hoped that Jennifer had a backup body.

The Tyrant

by Andrew Kurtz

I HAVE BEEN chosen by the people as a representative. Your tyrannical ways must cease!

"Executing women who are pregnant to avoid population increase, instead of getting an abortion, is monstrous!

"Publicly burning the old and sick alive because they are unproductive to society goes beyond inhumanity!

"The people chose you to govern us because we felt you would be beneficial to society; however, we were mistaken," Nicholas said as he removed a shotgun from his coat.

In an instant, a blue light disintegrated him, leaving only ash.

"Your requests have been denied," responded the computer system that ruled society.

Take It

by Jacqueline Moran Meyer

DAD AND I hid underneath a burned-out hovercraft, taking cover from the drone spraying us with hydrocarbon needles, which not only kill but turn the dead into fuel for the Cyborg's vehicles.

"Take it," Dad murmured after being hit.

When he died and transformed, I rummaged through his remains, swiping my hands over the slick oily goo, searching for his life's work. Finding the chip, I ran through the destroyed city clutching Dad's creation, humanity's lifesaver.

While sprinting towards the tunnel, the explosions around me intensify.

I will either reach and destroy the Cyborg's main computer grid or die trying.

System3011-01

by Meera Dandekar

THE DARK ALLEY felt more like home and reality hit me. What was the point of running? Nothing was going to make the sinking feeling of void leave my chest.

A robotic voice outed me; my location pinged on every broadcasting frequency.

The white, powder-coated, metallic subhuman flew in to arrest me. My crime didn't feel so serious anymore. It wasn't like it was alive—it's just metal.

I tased the machine and it broke down. A hologram flashed the best memories of my childhood. I read the label—System3011-01. The first of many.

My father was a great inventor.

Takeover

by Nerisha Kemraj

RUN, BILLY!" DAD said, trying to hold off the droids, a true rebel.

His father had prepped him for this, but Billy never thought the time would come.

"Mom! The machine men are here!" He slammed the front door and noticed the back door broken off its hinges. They were already inside.

"Billy!" Mom screamed from upstairs.

He ran into her open arms.

"Mom! The bunker. Now!"

Just then the bedroom door flew open, and out walked a droid—his mother's head in its hands, her blood dripping on the floor.

Billy gasped for air as the droid squeezed tighter.

Mighty Minions

by John H. Dromey

WHILE THE HOUSE shook like a road train crossing a speed hump, a visitor asked his host, "Is this an earthquake?"

"No, just some construction work being done next door. My neighbour conjured up several mythical creatures to help him. A satyr is inspecting the roof of his garage, for example. Being half goat, the hairy fellow's really surefooted."

"What's making that terrible racket and causing the ground to tremble?"

"He's also replacing his driveway. Since he's too cheap to rent a jackhammer to break up the asphalt, he's having that done by a couple of Golems on pogo sticks."

Remembrance

by S. Jade Path

REMEMBRANCE TECH'S TOUR group milled about. Servers wove smoothly between, offering golden, sparkling wines. The tour wouldn't begin until the last drop was licked from their lips—but they didn't know that.

While the wine did its work, Clio chatted with several clients, subtly priming.

Walk the facility, show off the memory extractors, storage options—a plash of something showy with nitrogen; the tech sold itself.

The clients sipped glasses of oblivion, signing away their memories, paying for the privilege.

Smiling, Clio tapped out a text.

Looking at her phone, Mnemosyne laughed. Rising, a new kind of Titan.

Huge Mistake

by Evan Baughfman

DR MORANIS GRINNED as his growth ray morphed a meagre fig into a monster atop the auditorium stage.

His demonstration complete, Moranis stepped beside the fruit, now the size of a Volkswagen Bug. "Imagine," he said, "an entire village fed for days on a single piece of locally-grown food."

His investors applauded. Cheered. Screamed.

For a parade of enlarged insects had suddenly burst free of the ripened orb, their residency inside unknown to Moranis until that very moment.

Gargantuan fig wasps swarmed stunned spectators.

Confused by people's colourful attire, the creatures attempted to pollinate every shrieking flower they could find.

Unfinished Business

by Mendel Mire

YOU SEE NOW why we need your help, Father?" Jack asked.

The priest wiped the vomit from his lips, surveying the carnage in the town square. Some buildings had been tossed across the street. Others obliterated entirely. The bodies of townsfolk were smeared across the rubble, like a bloody lacquer of skin, flesh, and bone. It was all too clear why the famous Jack the Giant Killer had sought his assistance.

"Perhaps we should have foreseen this," Jack continued. "Giants have souls too. It was just a matter of time before my work would give rise to a giant poltergeist."

Gaze Upon a Mountain Face

by Steven Holding

PANTING, WE REACHED the summit of the hill. My guide gestured towards the horizon. The stunning mountain range snatched my breath away even further.

"They call that ridge 'The Sleeping Giants',"

I could see why. Trapped within its topography were familiar looking shapes: monstrous, slumbering creatures.

"Legend say it's the Nephilim… Spawn of fallen angels, waiting to be called to paradise…"

Suddenly, I stumbled, as the ground surrounding us shook.

Earthquake? A landslide?

A chorus of a thousand trumpets echoed as the peak before us split open.

The dreaming beasts had been awoken.

And God have mercy…

They looked hungry.

How Long to Hide

by Joe Buckley

S O HARD TO hide at this size. Even harder to protest innocence. The littles never want to talk. They never give up the chase. They swarm and bite and buzz. He cannot hear a word, but he knows the sound of hate.

So easy to run at this size. Leaping bounds and stretching strides. But that only hastens the hunt.

So tempting to turn at this size. To swat and crush and snarl, to give them the guilt they want.

But that only swells the sting. So run. Hide. Try again. Until either they understand, or he deigns to war.

The Cure

by K.W. Reeds

I LOVE YOU," she'd said, with eyes so sad I wanted to take her in my arms.

"But it can't be," I'd replied, though it burned my heart. "We're so different, you and I."

She'd scowled, the action wrinkling her nose into cuteness.

"What if I promise not to share special kisses with you?" she'd offered with a sniff.

I wanted so badly for her to share my life. But the sacrifice was huge. Especially for her.

She gazed up at me, smiling lovingly, from beneath watery lashes as I finished the stitch that would seal her zombie lips forever.

Means to an End

by Avery Hunter

MUST YOU MAKE that infernal noise?" the domovoy grumbled.

"I'm hungry," the kikimora replied, a scowl on her face.

"Can't you just raid the fridge like a normal house spirit?"

"Can't. I'm stuck."

"What do you mean, you're stuck?"

"I'm wedged behind the stove."

The domovoy tutted but quieted when one of the Kobliska children came in.

The kikimora continued her mouse-like *eeks*, and the child leaned over the stove to see what was making the noise.

A snarl, a screech, a mashing of bones, the dripping of blood.

Silence.

"I'm not hungry anymore," a satisfied kikimora said then belched.

Butchered

by D.M. Burdett

I'M HUNGRY. I know there's food…well, I say food, but it's just some swill the farmer's left in the trough for us…but it's not what I'm used to. I can't eat it.

I suppose, at some point, my hunger will overtake the feelings of disgust, and the mush of soybean meal and moulding fruit will become tempting. But I can't eat that shit. At least not yet. But I guess I'll get hungry enough sooner or later.

The other girls he has confined in this concrete prison with me all think the same way too. We grumble amongst ourselves quietly, scared in case the farmer hears us. It's hard to tell which version of Farmer John we'll get if we interrupt him while he's working; the nice one who brings us delicious food treats, or the one who yells and shouts, yanks us from our straw beds as we squeal and cry, knowing we'll never see our sisters again.

So we stay as quiet as we can, mooching around in the straw, keeping a low profile lest we get chosen for whatever deranged antics the farmer might have in store for us.

But, sweet Jesus, I'm hungry. My stomach grumbles and I hunt around the bottom of the pen for any leftovers from our last 'real' meal. The delightful smells have leached into the concrete and my tongue salivates at the memory of all the titbits we've been thrown in the past.

My nose swipes against something and my eyes widen when I see the finger. The gold ring, yellow sapphire muddied and dull, reminds me of the owner who had come into the barn a few days before. She had screamed and wept, keening like a banshee. It had been so frightening! We'd huddled together in the corner, scrambling over each other so as not to be closest to all the noise, panting and shaking with fear.

Later, the woman had quietened down, and we tiptoed to the gate of our concrete jail and looked out across the row of meat hooks, watching Farmer John as he worked.

"Alright now, Alice," Farmer John said to the unconscious woman as he lifted her chin to inspect a deep gash across her forehead. "There was no need for all that rowdy palaver, my dear," he mumbled. But Alice didn't respond. Blood poured from the cut, traced a red river across her cheeks, and pooled under her head.

Farmer John took scissors to Alice's clothing, slicing up the sleeves and legs so everything fell away to reveal bruised and broken skin, reds and purples merging together into a mottled pattern of pain.

Tying thick rope around her ankles, he attached her to one of the meat hooks and raised her up high above the blood-catching trough, her arms dangling loosely and her damp hair dripping blood onto the steel surface.

She came to a little then, her eyes opening slowly as she swung like a pendulum.

"Glad you could join us, Alice," he said with a chuckle. "For a minute there, I thought you were going to be unkosher. What a waste that would have been."

Alice, swinging slowly, confusion furrowing her brow, moaned softly.

That's when Farmer John got out the leather pouch; the one that contained his very best knives. He hesitated just a moment, and then made his selection. Holding it up, he watched the light from the windows glint on the sharp edge, and then, in one quick movement, sliced precisely across Alice's neck, severing her oesophagus, trachea, carotid arteries and jugular vein in one smooth action.

Alice jerked once, eyes wide, and then gurgled quietly as crimson fluid splashed across the trough below her. After just a few moments, the spasms stopped, and the swinging slowed.

We watched it all from the safety of our pen, peering through the bars of the gate; the precision of the butchery as he carved up the joints, the artistry in the removal of the offal and fatty bits.

And, oh the smells! I'm reminded of them now as I lick the ringed finger.

And after he'd finished packaging all the meat, that's when we got our treat; the head and hands, the feet and fat.

So utterly delicious!

And, of course, when we'd finished, there was hardly a scrap left—us piggies are not known for leaving leftovers—just the shiny, stripped-clean skull abandoned in the corner, and this little morsel that got forgotten in the feast.

Yum!

My Ex-boyfriend

by Delfina Bonuchi

HE THRUSTS AND grunts; his weekly treat.

But I only feel the wind teasing my hair, sunshine on my face.

I listen to the trees; malevolent, they whisper his name.

He finishes, pulls up his pants.

"You'll always be my girl," he says, caressing my bone-white cheek, pressing a wet kiss to bloated lips. He pushes my body back into the shallow grave, tenderly re-covers my swollen, black flesh.

He stands when the job is done, leans against the tree. *My* tree.

Bark separates, he falls inside; bones splinter and skin rips.

You'll always be my girl, my tree whispers.

Intelligent Life

by N.E. Rule

K HIIKI STROKES THE silky hair through the cage bars, pleading, "Dad, I can't choose."

"Darling, we can't get both. They're cute, but when they mature, they won't like this handling." Tsts nods at his spawn tickling the female's belly. "This male will grow hair everywhere, it needs constant grooming." What Tsts can't mention is their mating; how it's noisy and messy.

The male's blue eyes peer up under long lashes. "Can it understand us?" She clicks.

"No," Tsts clicks back. Then, he can't resist extending his tentacle to pet the tiny human. He smiles as it curls into a ball.

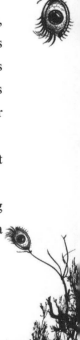

Sleep Under the Stars

by Bernardo Villela

IT WAS A marvellous night to sleep under the stars.

Soon, I awoke. The moonlight seemed wrong somehow. Rubbing sleep from my eyes, I saw massive branches asway. Not branches but antennae, leading to a gargantuan ovoid shadow blotting out the moon. I couldn't be seeing what I thought I was seeing, could I? Moonlit mandibles confirmed my fears: It was a cockroach towering above the centuries-old oak I'd camped under.

I ran. The light changed. Glancing skyward, I saw an intrusion of flying cockroaches swooping down. I tripped, pain rose, I'd lost my foot. Maimed, they started feasting.

Sacrifice

by Chris Bannor

THEY TOWERED ABOVE us, blocking out the sun in their magnificence. We tried to fight, but how do you stop a creature so massive it engulfs your house with a single footstep?

The government made mechanical monstrosities to combat the invaders, but the damage grew worse. The aliens came to subjugate, not destroy, but in our fight for freedom, we destroyed ourselves far better than they.

Now it's up to us. We have small teams ready with explosives. We have the will to survive.

But in a suicide mission to save the world, do we have the will to die?

Unclaimed and Quiet

by Miriam H. Harrison

THEY HAD WARNED us of giants, and so we watched for the swaying of trees, the sudden flight of birds. Yet all around us were silent forests and barren hills. From the highest of these summits, we could see even more of this land, unclaimed and quiet.

"Have you ever seen a place so still?"

My captain snorted. "Better to face stillness than giants. Set the flag; we'll make camp."

The silence loomed large as I readied the flag. But as I pushed it into the ground and blood spurted up, the hill beneath us lurched and bellowed in rage.

Beware of the Talls

by John Lane

BORN IN A pan of green beef, seventy-five of us reached maturity in two to three days.

We laughed when Mom warned that "talls" wanted us dead. Our compound eyes and thin wings could evade them. Or so we thought.

The "talls" caught us while we rubbed our six legs on grooves of wood. They looked like their heads touched the white drywall sky.

Then… *WHACK!*

I watched the large flat plastic crush my brothers until mangled thoraxes littered the wood. Smell of pheromones lingered.

Only I survived.

I will never forget what the "talls" called their death weapon.

Flyswatter.

Glassman Had His Reasons

by C.L. Steele

HUNCHED OVER, HIS glass head slid across the ceiling tiles of her office. She cowered in the corner. She could see through his pristine cyan outline—a glass man. His protracted fingers extracted her with an ease that whispered experience. She trembled in the valley of his palm. He examined her with his laser-blue eyes, each pass a deepening CT Scan.

He whispered, "Globe." Molten glass coagulated into a glass ball. Trembling, she found herself sealed inside the globe with sand and a towering willow tree. "Why?" she screamed as he tossed her into the Atlantic. "Because I must, dear."

One More for the Road

by Blaise Langlois

ROUTE 37 AT night is a lonely stretch. My eyelids feel the weight of sleep, but the next exit promises 24-hour coffee.

The car lot, bathed in a sick, yellow light, is practically deserted. I order a coffee and venture round back to use the restroom, but a foul smell makes my eyes water, giving me second thoughts. Flies buzz, insistent, drawing my gaze to where a trailer stands, rear doors ajar. Something oily and slick in the moonlight, pools on the asphalt beneath. Heavy hands grasp my shoulders.

"Always room for one more," a thick voice whispers from behind.

Little Truck Stop on the Prairie

by Jameson Grey

GUNNARS DINER [SIC] reeked of rank meat—like the fridge was broken or the sous-chef hadn't checked the expiry dates.

Sous-chef? Marilyn wondered. *Did middle-of-nowhere greasy spoons even have them?*

Her Freightliner was the only rig in the lot. Marilyn was beat, and hours from the next truck stop, but the smell convinced her groaning stomach it no longer wanted to eat.

"Coffee, please," she said. "To go."

The waitress smiled, yelling to the kitchen. "We got a lady trucker, Gunnar!"

Gunnar emerged, his apron stained blood-red.

His cleaver gleamed. *Gunnar* gleamed.

"Excellent, I ain't cooked a lady in weeks."

The Lay-by

by Liam Hogan

IDON'T LIKE to stop. The cab fulfils my needs, from somewhere to sleep, to food and drink: coffee and instant noodles, a travelling kettle serving for both.

But you can't resist a call of nature forever.

No need for a truck stop or gas station, not when there's woodland either side.

By day, the lay-by would be busy with dog walkers, in summer with hikers and family picnics. On a damp April night, it's utterly empty.

Not dark though; not with a full moon peeking between the clouds.

I unleash a howl even before my paws hit the ground.

Scrapple

by Warren Benedetto

I 'LL HAVE THE scrapple," I said.

The waitress glanced at the fist-sized bruise on my arm, then at Mike. I nodded. She jotted on her pad.

"Coffee." Mike thrust the menu at the waitress. "Black."

The waitress disappeared into the kitchen. Through the swinging doors, I saw her hand my order to the cook. He read it, then looked out at me. Eye contact. A small nod.

"What's even in scrapple?" Mike sneered.

"Pork bits," I explained. "Lips, nips, and assholes."

The cook emerged from the kitchen. He approached Mike from behind, meat cleaver in hand.

"Mostly assholes," I added.

Black Dog

by L.J. McLeod

HE'D HEARD OTHER truckers talk about the black dog, but this was ridiculous. The fluffy mutt between him and his truck could've fit in his hand. It cocked its head to one side, eyes filling with white light. As it started towards him, he wondered where it had come from. Those eyes seemed to keep getting bigger. The light was mesmerising. It broke into a run, so close that those eyes were all he could see. Its mouth opened and a loud honk rang out. He woke up just in time to see the other truck bearing down on him.

Safe Haven

by Michelle Brett

CALL AN AMBULANCE. Someone's been hurt."

Marcus burst through the doors of the gas station; the bright lights irritating his eyes. He laid Mary down on the tiles and pressed his jacket against her leg.

"It's okay, Mary. I've found help."

But she only mumbled in reply, her eyes closed and her face drenched in sweat. The blood, having already soaked through the fabric, now pooled onto the floor.

Marcus called again.

"Hello?"

No response.

Then finally, footsteps. A sign of life. Marcus felt a wave of relief.

Until another noise followed, metal against tiles. The dragging of an axe.

Overgrown

by Jodi Jensen

WOULD YOU LOOK at this…" Ignoring the weeds growing in an abandoned truck at the derelict rest stop, Randall slid into the driver's seat and gripped the gear shifter. "It's so cool."

A movement by his elbow caught his attention, and he turned to see a broad green leaf wrap around his arm. Razor-sharp edges cut into his flesh and blood dribbled down his wrist as another leaf wrapped around his leg.

Vines twisted around his chest, pinning him in the seat as a massive pod opened from the steering wheel.

Gleaming rows of bloody teeth gnashed, swallowing his screams.

Full Service

by Andrew McDonald

IT WAS 3 a.m. when the 18-wheeler pulled into Phil's twenty-four seven rest stop. Phil's was a massive and all-encompassing set up—restaurant and store, gas pumps, car wash, efficiency units and showers—basically everything a trucker needs.

Pulling up to the car wash area, an attendant ran to the truck and hopped up onto the wide step. The driver asked for the premium full service and went to shower and change his bloody clothes.

The attendant removed the mangled corpse from the cab, to be disposed of later, before doing a deep clean. The driver tipped well, as usual.

The Helpful Attendant

by Stephen Johnson

THE NEON BULBS flickered, casting a foreboding crimson shadow outside the isolated truck stop. I pulled to a stop on fumes, staring inside at the solitary light portraying only the back of a head visible in the store. Cautiously, I walked in and entered a surreal silence that engulfed me. I turned to the register to see a mangled bloody severed head staring back at me positioned on the counter with a devious smile placed on its lips. I felt a putrid cold breath slide across my neck and a gravelly voice whisper in my ear, "Can I help you?"

Last Words

by John Lane

WITH ZOMBIE APOCALYPSE nonstop on mainstream news, Don, terminal manager for Moe's Truck Stop, unplugged the television.

Greg Watson staggered inside, repeatedly mumbling, "I can't do this anymore."

Outside stood Greg's reefer trailer—the constant shaking was a red flag. Inhuman moans reverberated throughout the parking lot.

When Don walked over, he noticed the trailer side's convex impressions of human-sized hands.

He peeked through the small rectangular door. Four stiff and slow, pale figures in torn clothes kept walking into walls.

Back at Moe's, Don handed the keys back to Greg. Don's last words? "I can't do this anymore, either."

The Diner

by Tracy Davidson

MANAGER AND MONSTER struck a truce.

It was easy enough, in an out-of-town diner, to drug an on-foot drifter or a hitcher in between rides. Easier still to escort them out back, leave them unconscious in a dark corner, hidden from the highway.

Like this vagrant, tonight.

The manager retreats. He watched once. Never again.

The monster smells fresh meat. It's hungry. No prey comes near his territory anymore. It prefers human flesh anyway, however seldom it appears.

It bites…slashes…gorges on gut and gore.

Before morning, the manager will clear the mess away. As a good brother should.

Bartender Lobotomist

by Jodie Angell

A SHARP WIND whistled through the forest. The abandoned bar's shutters rattled. Leaves fluttered through the open door to join the broken glass. Fluorescent light flickered.

A blown transformer snuffed the last of the light.

The bartender downed a shot of Tequila, then descended into the cellar; her makeshift practise.

She grabbed her finest knitting needle and twisted it between her fingers.

Her captive fought against his leather restraints—his screams muffled by the wad of cloth in his mouth.

She clamped his head against the chair and pressed the needle into his eye. "This may hurt just a little."

Fleeting Fame

by Colleen Anderson

DAIYU GASPED. THIS rare discovery—a complete warrior's burial chamber—ensured her career trajectory.

She pulled a carved jade amulet off the leathery mummy's chest. The lantern flickered, the chamber echoing with more than falling water. Howling whooshed up the tunnel. Misty apparitions sliced her like freezing knives as she tried to block their access to the sarcophagus.

Slashing with archaeological picks did nothing as they dived into the shrivelled warrior's form. Clawlike fingers twitched.

Taking the lantern oil, she doused the rousing body. Daiyu dropped a match, and flames cleansed everything, consuming the zombie.

There would be other finds.

Where the Dead Things Are

by L.J. McLeod

WENDY HATED THE morgue. As the hospital's night cleaner, it fell to her to keep it spotless. But that didn't make it any less creepy. The silence felt heavy and the smell of cold corpse hung in the air as she mopped. Tonight's storm only made it feel more oppressive. Lights flickered periodically and she could hear the thunder rumble through the walls. Her heart began to race at the thought of being trapped down here in a power outage. Sudden darkness filled the room, making nightmare reality. A cold hand seized her shoulder.

"Don't worry. You're never alone here."

A Nice Long Soak

by Mike Rader

I HEARD THEM climbing the stairs. Tourists. Mayday Hills Asylum attracted the morbid to Beechworth.

I waited on the second floor of that Victorian pile. In the bathroom. Where each tub has a sturdy wooden cover. Back in the day, only an inmate's head was visible when the attendants poured scalding hot or freezing cold water over the poor unfortunate locked inside. Shock treatment, they called it.

Two kids entered. Gawking.

"Bet they screamed," the boy said.

"Gross," the girl said.

I smashed their heads together, bundled them into a bath, locked the lid.

Boiling hot water did the rest.

Dared

by S. Jade Path

HER FRIENDS HAD dared her to enter the ward. She was young, brash, invincible—foolish. Her breath chuffed out. *Teenage pride.*

The wind wended through the shattered halls; a remnant of laughter, and a memory of screams.

A shriek of tortured metal and the scent of old blood rise into the air where her hands settled on one of the bed frames rusting in the gloaming.

Her eyes skimmed the scarred floors, littered with detritus.

In the corner, empty liquor bottles surround a wilted mattress. Mostly hidden by a shred of faded blue denim, her skull stares back at her.

Hospital Corridors

by Dale Parnell

THE NURSE AT the main desk said my father had been moved; G-ward, at the other end of the hospital. I had missed visiting hours, but they said the rules were relaxed for certain patients. I knew what they meant.

It's surprising how quiet a hospital can be. Long corridors with cold fluorescent tubes flickering overhead. Naked, abandoned beds, stripped of warmth and comfort.

Once or twice I thought I heard footsteps, but I never saw anyone.

When I finally arrived at my father's ward, the duty nurse gave me the news, and I understood whose footsteps I had heard.

Where Angels Fear

by Kimberly Rei

THE CHURCHYARD TREMBLED at night. Pauly said that wasn't possible. Pauly was full of shit. Stand off the property and it was fine, but so much as one toe over the edge and there it was. The ground was afraid. The old small church was scared right down to it's last nail. If you listened closely, if you could get past the trees rustling, you could hear the pews tremble.

No one had attended mass there in decades. Centuries, maybe.

But they still buried their dead on that land. I know. I tended the graves. And I felt them quiver.

Dilapidated

by Alyson Hasson

THE DOORKNOB SLIPPED from her grasp as the oversized emerald door swung open, exposing the darkness within. Her heart pounded—the door should have been locked. Frigid water encompassed her feet as she stepped into the void. The walls leaned inwards around her, thick moss coating their surface.

The door slammed shut, casting her into blinding darkness. Her breath caught in her throat. The pungent scent of mildew filled her nostrils, and tinnitus stifled her hearing. A shrill scream escaped her lips as waterlogged walls draped around her. They bore down onto her, sucking the oxygen out of her lungs.

The Burial Plot

by Susmita Ramani

WAKING, I'VE NEVER experienced such absolute darkness and silence. Peeling apart my clasped hands, I feel around. Above me and to my sides is wood. Below me is satin. I smell fresh earth. I can't stop sweating and shaking, feeling waves of heat like I'm being dipped into boiling water. I take deep breaths and hold them, focusing on each inhale, to avoid hyperventilating. I have an hour, maybe two. Positioning my hands, palms out, in front of my chest, I press upward. Nothing. Again. After some amount of time, I hear a sound: wood splintering.

It's like angels singing.

St Mary's Hospital for Insane

by Jodie Angell

SOULS NEVER LEAVE St Mary's Hospital for Insane. They wander the hallways, linger in the mirrors for too long, and hide in the walls.

Their screams still echo against the high stone pillars. Two-hundred dead still roam the grounds, eternally searching for peace that won't come.

A broken doll lies on the wooden floorboards beside an old hair comb—belongings of a girl long since passed. Moonlight cascades in through her old bedroom window, illuminating the leather restraints and the sheets still stained with blood.

Her face appears in the shattered mirror. Blood spills from her eyes as she grins.

Wasn't a Ghost

by Evan Baughfman

THE DOOR CREAKED open. Kellan took a deep breath and stepped into the shadowy classroom.

Inside, no children chuckled. No teacher taught. Silence suffused like creeping fog.

Cobwebs clung to ceiling corners. Darkness enveloped desks.

Toppled chairs and abandoned assignments lay scattered on the floor.

Very little was as Kellan remembered. He'd been a student here years before.

As he approached his old seat, he heard soft cries. Figures huddled, hidden in gloom.

Kellan's rifle lifted toward the trembling targets.

"Boo," he said, though he wasn't a ghost.

He'd become something far more monstrous the moment he returned to school.

The Bus Shelter

by Tracy Davidson

NO LOCALS USE this bus shelter at night. Few use it in the daytime. Something about these three urine-stained, graffiti-marked walls drives them away.

Some smell decay. Some hear voices. Some see shadows dance. And some feel sharp slashes across backs and bellies, though no wounds appear.

Such sensations deepen in the dark. Only out-of-towners stop here then.

Like this one. He looks lost. Lonely. We like them lonely. They don't get missed.

He shivers, despite the humidity. My invisible sisters surround him, begin their games. I let them play. It's been a while.

Tomorrow, another shadow will dance here.

Down the Basement

by Jean Martin

MY HUSBAND ALWAYS said I was foolish. "There's nothing in the basement at night that isn't there in the daytime."

Our basement is a cellar, not a carpeted play space—even with the lights on, you can't see what's in the corners when it's dark.

I don't like it. It scares me.

My husband went down the basement last night to get a screwdriver.

I found him this morning at the foot of the stairs, with his throat torn out.

Once the estate is settled, I'm selling the house. Meanwhile, I'm living at my sister's—she doesn't have a basement.

Passage for Two

by N.E. Rule

SANDRA'S KNUCKLES WHITEN on the steering wheel as the wipers whip back and forth. Glancing into the rearview mirror, she gasps as a man leans towards her. She swerves to the shoulder and brakes. She reaches for the door, but his bony fingers dig into her collarbone.

"Who are you?!" she cries.

"A guide to the afterlife."

"I'm not dead!"

"I'm here for the body you have in the trunk." Then he nods to the passenger seat. "He's your guide."

A beast forms beside her. Screaming, she jerks free of his grasp as the transport truck hits her car head-on.

After the Ascent

by Evan Baughfman

WALTER ROSE ABOVE his corpse. His spirit approached a widening glow.

Amazing! An otherworldly oasis opening up itself just for him! Sunlight! Beach! Palm trees!

Walter smiled at the sound of lost loved ones' laughter. His philanthropic life would soon reunite him with his mother, his father!

The glow extinguished.

Walter plummeted. Pleaded.

He fell back into flesh.

Injected chemicals had begun to restart and preserve his brain.

Walter screamed at his doctors to release him. His mouth wouldn't move.

Walter, trapped inside his skull, was stuffed into his cryochamber, a sub-zero casket he now certainly regretted ever paying for.

Clairvoyance

by L.T. Ward

THE CANDLELIGHT REFRACTED within the glass of Antonia's crystal ball—all a part of her clairvoyant's show.

"Does he forgive me?" the man across from her asked.

She stared into the sepia light, her hands waving a practiced dance above. With her bare feet beneath her long skirt, Antonia tugged the hem. The metal balls sewn within clacked twice.

"He forgives you."

The man sank back into his seat, sighing. As he pulled the money owed from his wallet, she asked, "Why would a good man like you need forgiveness?"

An icy chill whispered into her ear, "For my murder."

The Crimson Room

by Stephen Johnson

MY EYES OPENED to a quiet darkness. *Strange, I don't remember coming into the den.* I saw a fiery crimson glow emanating from the open doorway to my living room. I tried to enter but the crimson wall repulsed me back.

Confused, I noticed a body spread across the floor. Blood was sprayed across the back wall and pooled under the lifeless head. My eyes locked with the woman standing over the dead man. Terror filled her face, and she dropped the knife, looking down nervously at the body on the floor.

"No, it can't be. I just killed you."

In the Dark

by L.J. McLeod

DARK. COLD. HER breath comes in shallow gasps. The air tastes stale. A hint of rot tickles at her nose. There is no movement, everything is still. She closes her eyes and opens them again. There is no change in the infinite blackness. Her hands are trapped, her feet bound tight. The feel of walls presses in all around her. With an effort she pulls herself back, away from the vision she has seen in her crystal ball. She looks across the table at the eager, young tourist. He leans forward expectantly.

"So, what do you see in my future?"

Mercy's Harp

by Jodie Angell

MERCY'S FINGERS PLUCKED the harp strings, sensing the nearby souls in their final moments before death.

She overlooked the man, unconscious in his armchair.

The room filled with graceful harmony, and the music rose to a crescendo.

A tear rolled from her eyes as a final breath escaped his mouth. A silvery whisp floated from between his lips—his soul now free from the shackles of life.

The music halted, and Mercy reached out her hands to cradle the drifting soul. It disappeared as another spirit called for her.

The room snapped shut, and another materialised. Her songs began again.

Double Betrayal

by Jaycee Durand

CLARA TRAILED HER fingertips over the mirror's chilled glass, her heart tripping at the beckoning reflection.

Identical green eyes—but Debra's derisive smirk.

Impossible!

We are one. Without me, there is no you. Come.

Always belittling. Always controlling.

But how do you live on when your other half is dead?

Clara sagged before her sister's stare… and clasped the hand Debra slipped through the rippling mirrored surface as if from the depths of dark waters.

Snatched into frigid, swirling inkiness, Clara whimpered in fright.

Debra threw a vile and triumphant grin to the shadowed presence.

She's yours, Master. Feast well.

The Messenger

by Constantine E. Kiousis

"THIS IT?" JENNIFER asked as she pointed at the suburban house opposite them in the dimly lit street.

The pale girl standing next to her nodded. Huffing, Jennifer crossed the street, walked up to the front porch, slid a sealed envelope under the door, and knocked before trotting away.

Soon, the girl's mother would be finding out it was their neighbour that killed her daughter, burying her body in his backyard.

"We good?" Jennifer asked the child.

Smiling, the phantom dissipated into the cold night.

"You're welcome!" Jennifer exclaimed. "Ghosts and their unfinished business," she muttered.

Being a medium sucked.

Witching Hour

by S. Jade Path

THE VEIL IS always thinnest on Samhain.

Kylie cast her spell with trembling fingers, before stepping through the fluttering, gossamer threads and into a world of glittering wonder.

Just a quick peek can't hurt, she thought.

***

Distantly, sonorous chimes announced the passing of midnight. The stars winked out as one, and with a snap, the veil turned to rubber.

Kylie pushed at the barrier with her foot. It gave as it always did, bouncing back as soon as her foot moved. She flopped against the wall, a scream of frustration echoing around the opulent room—now her gilded cage.

Something Old

by Susan Vita

ROSIA NAVIGATED THE aisle alone. She came from a line of widows, but it was poppycock that the veil was cursed. Her candlelight satin dress suited the heirloom and hid her growing belly.

The groom took her hand, and tears slid down her cheeks when she saw him. He lifted the veil, but cringed away from the crumbling, putrid flesh where his young wife's pretty face should have been. He fell to the ground, clutching his chest.

As he inhaled his last breath, Rosie's face went back to normal.

Her sisters embraced her and walked her out of the chapel.

Ebenezer's Corner

by Raven Isobel Plum

WHEN MY DOG, Ebenezer, stared at 'nothing,' I always assumed he heard something outside the house.

Yet, each day, he spent more time guarding the shadowy corner, increasingly transfixed, not allowing us near.

When Miss Jeanie, the psychic, came, she pointed to that exact spot with bangled arms, saying, "You have an extra inhabitant here."

Unsettled, we followed her advice. We left out a chair and sometimes a cup of tea. Burnt sage and prayed. Peace offerings. It might've worked.

Miss Jeanie neglected to tell us ghosts can be dangerous.

Now when my dog stares, it's me he's staring at.

Snow Flower

by Dorian J. Sinnott

IT WAS WHEN the silver moonlight touched the freshly fallen snow that I saw you again. Out amongst the birches and pines. The frigid night. The dead of winter.

How it ate away at your blued lips and flesh. Gnawing down to the cold bone. Clinging to your lashes—painted white. Beneath the shower of snowflakes, I bid you farewell.

For the last time…

***

My garden of ghosts, how much it's grown. Buried bones beneath the frozen earth. Lost. Forgotten.

Yet every winter, upon the first snowfall, still I find you. Like an airy perennial. Blossoming under the winter moon.

Show Time

by Liam Hogan

IT'S THE SAME every night: the waiting, otherworldly forms, thronging the hallway, packing the stairs.

Almost the same. Different individuals. He tries not to see their faces, or their strange attire. He'd avoid them altogether, but the waves of disappointment linger, tainting his home.

He hurries through the ordeal, looking neither left nor right as he passes between them. The buzz on his appearance, the fusillade of flashes...and always, as he escapes through the wall that hadn't been there in his time, the same theatrical announcement:

"And that, folks, is why *this* is the most haunted house in England!"

Safe and Alone

by Gary Smith Jr.

THE SIZE AND strength of the house impresses me, for the thousandth time. Reaching the massive door, I stare into the camera.

"What are you doing here, Julie? I can't let you in."

Shuffling from foot to foot, I glance back towards the street. "Please," I beg, "I'll never make it home."

I wait.

An electrical buzz and click from the door.

I step inside.

The siren sounds.

The purge has started.

As my best friend pushes the door shut behind me, I pull the knife from the back of my pants.

This year I will be safe and alone.

A Deadly Lesson

by Andrew Kurtz

THE COLLEGE PROFESSOR walked into the classroom carrying two pizza boxes.

"Three hours from now, the Purge will begin. Once a year, our government allows murder to be legal for twelve hours.

"Some of you enjoy shooting people in the head, causing the brain matter to spill out. Others prefer slitting throats and watching the victim choke in their own blood. Cracking skulls with a baseball bat or burning people alive are popular too.

"I brought some pizza to celebrate, dig in," he told the class, knowing that the deadly poison in the food would take effect in three hours.

The Blood Purge

by J.M. Faulkner

PALE-SKINNED GIRL RUNS. Pale-skinned girl trips. Pale-skinned girl shields her eyes from the streetlamp that throws a shadow on my shoulders.

"Please, d-don't hurt me."

Sigh… If we elders didn't cull the young, vampires would spill onto the streets like mice. There wouldn't be an ounce of blood to share.

I tell her, "We purge annually. Your sire should have kept you safe."

She winces. Tiny fangs protrude over her trembling bottom lip. "Sire didn't warn me."

"Then he wants you dead as much as—"

Thump.

A stake in my chest.

She says, "Now the young purges the old."

Rule Three

by N.E. Rule

WE'VE NOW COVERED the two rules to survive The Purge." Stanley announces. Taking his eyes away from the road, he smiles at Judy.

"One, find shelter as far from the city as possible." He pulls up to the log cabin.

"Two, partner up with someone you trust." He leans over to kiss her. Judy turns so his kiss lands on her cheek.

A woman sits up from from the blanketed backseat holding a gun to his temple. "What about rule three?" Stanley stills. "Make sure your girlfriend doesn't find out you're married." She winks at Judy, then pulls the trigger.

Heavy Lifting

by Marion Lougheed

DAMIEN HUFFED AS he worked his shovel. The night was cold against his flushed cheeks.

He laid a diamond necklace on his growing pile of goods. Though dusty from the grave, the diamonds glittered like teeth.

One grave left to pillage. Nothing valuable here, only a broken pipe beside a grinning skull. A rat poked its snout through an eye socket.

"Hey," the groundskeeper shouted. "Grave robbing's illegal!"

"Not on purge night."

"Ah, that's right." A shot rang out and blood bloomed across Damien's chest. As he fell, a hand scooped up his collection. "Thanks for doing the heavy lifting."

Whose Purge Is It Anyway?

by Tracy Davidson

H E HAD WAITED months for this night. Months of patient planning, honing weaponry skills, studying his primary target. During the purge, he would happily kill anyone crossing his path. He wanted one person in particular. Not just to kill, but torture—punishment for deserting him.

He knew her well. Knew where she would run and hide. Becoming an instant widower would be quicker and cheaper than divorce.

The alarm sounded. Heavily armed, he stepped out of his front door. Barely saw the machete gleam in moonlight, before it buried itself in his chest.

His wife… widow… knew him too well.

Breeders

by Bernardo Villela

THE POINT OF the Culling is Scrooge-like: "decrease the surplus population." Other laws can be broken in the hopes people die.

My band of sharpshooters and I take this responsibility very seriously. Year-round we study those who ought not be, who oughtn't deplete natural resources, who oughtn't procreate. We know where they live, where they work, where they drink.

Our allies have infiltrated the bars they thought safe.

The night has come, prone we lie on the ridge, guns poised.

Drunk, they waddle out like wounded ducks. Easy prey.

Our kills are exponential as we rid the world of breeders.

Clean Sheet

by Pauline Yates

THE WESTRIDGE FOOTBALL team walks the streets, searching for victims. The pre-season tradition, allowing players to purge their sexual desires in a one-night fucking frenzy, has resulted in four consecutive premiership wins. No one reports the pack rapes, the deaths. All this town sees is the trophy.

Not me. I have different purge in mind. From my bedroom window, I aim a rifle at the team. Tommy leads the pack. We've shared a kiss, talked about a future. He promised he wouldn't partake. He lied. They all lied; town expectation their excuse.

My excuse? I hate football. Why complicate things?

Liar, Liar

by S. Jade Path

FRANTICALLY PULLING AGAINST her bonds, Halle pleaded, "Please. Please, no." Her voice jumped an octave, "Why are you doing this?"

"Why?" I crooned, grinning beneath the Purge mask.

I splashed petrol around her, watched it soak into the scattered books—kindling for her pyre. I stepped close, and Halle's panic-filled struggles intensified.

I grabbed her head, pushed torn pages and rags into her mouth, held them in place with phone cords.

Then I whispered, "Liar, liar."

Her eyes, filling with recognition and guilt, turned to horror as my match fell.

Liar, liar pants on fire. Hanging by a telephone wire!

A Quiet Word with the Boss

by L.J. McLeod

THE BLOOD WAS still warm where it coated her skin. Crimson beads dripped slowly from her hair. She had even gotten some in her mouth; it tasted salty and metallic. When Tegan had seen her boss's light on, she had only wanted to have a quiet word with her.

There was no one else around. It was the perfect time to bring up her completely reasonable complaint. But the woman was so stubborn and pig-headed! A soft noise made her turn, the scissors still gripped tight in her hand.

"Enjoying the Purge, hey?" the night cleaner asked.

"Enjoying the what?"

Home Protection

by Joel R. Hunt

THE STREETS WERE full of thugs and murderers. Rebecca had begged him to stay home, but her apartment block was crawling with them. He couldn't risk anything happening to her. He needed to be with her. Protect her.

He charged down the corridor and hammered on her door.

"Rebecca! Rebec—"

Bang.

A bullet tore through the door. Pain exploded in his chest. He collapsed.

Rebecca had mistaken him for a thug. She'd shot him.

With his last breath, he prayed she wouldn't blame herself.

At least she was safe.

***

Beyond the door, Rebecca's new boyfriend grinned at her.

"Got him."

Family is a Solid Foundation

by Dale Parnell

HARRIS STARED DOWN into the freshly dug foundations, watching his husband's body spasmodically twitch. Harris reversed the cement truck into place and, after whispering a solemn prayer, started to pour the wet cement. He hadn't wanted it to end like this, but Andre had refused to share his inheritance, and Harris had so many debts.

With the foundations filled, Harris switched off the truck. A sudden pinch at the back of his neck made Harris turn, coming face-to-face with his eldest son.

"Sorry, Dad." Casey shrugged, pocketing the hypodermic needle, "but you're not the only one with debts to pay."

No One to Call for Help

by Stephen Johnson

THE BAT PELTED down again across the defenceless man's back as chaos ran through the streets on the celebration of *No Law Night.*

"If you don't stop, I will call the police!" The frightened man threatened with the most confident voice he could muster, raising his arms in a futile attempt to block the next strike.

"Go ahead," the man snarled behind the bloody plastic mask.

"I am the police," the man spoke as he lifted the mask and tossed an old picture of the man smiling in the paper with the headline: Local Owner Kills Cop—Released on Technicality.

Emergency Broadcast

by Liam Hogan

THIS IS NOT a test.

This is the commencement of the Purge. Any crime, including murder, will be legal for the next twelve hours.

May I suggest some targets for you?

Jonathan Kinclair hiked the price of insulin fifty percent over the last year. Perhaps he deserves a visit?

Poisoned water in the poorer parts of our city? Councilwoman Eleanor Rodriguez should shoulder the blame and the punishment.

Then there's Governor Aldritch, who started this annual—

Ah. They've arrived at the studio. You get the idea, I hope. Time for me to sign off.

May God be with you all.

The Ridding

by Jameson Grey

AFTER LANDFALL, THEY rode westwards.

They had weapons; they had numbers. And they rode in the Lord's name. Each time the riders came across a settlement, they offered salvation. If the villagers didn't accept it, there were other means.

They hanged the men slowly—long enough for them to see what was done to their wives. When the riders were finished with the women, they slit their throats while the elder children watched.

The youngest, they took.

After the ridding, they moved on—raping and pillaging with impunity.

It was a new world, with new frontiers. New rules.

Their rules.

Escaping Inferno

by Renee Cronley

TONIGHT, YOUR LOCKED doors are about as useful as mine were that night you came to me. In my heart I know the scent of the gasoline I'm painting your house with inspires the same fear in you as the chloroform did in me.

A restraining order is not justice.

I don't have to live with you inside me anymore. *That* was like being dead.

When I strike the match, I come back to life. With a flick of my wrist, your hold on me goes ablaze and brings light to the darkness you forced on me.

Now I'm free.

Scratch

by Christy Brown

DAVE ADJUSTED THE backpack slung over his shoulder. He'd already discarded his college books into the backseat of his car and filled the pack with snacks, his hoodie, and a few other necessary provisions. The sun had set about two hours prior, but he continued to hike the interstate, looking to catch a ride into the next town. He'd watched three vehicles fly past—not much hope so far. He considered calling an Uber but decided to stick it out just a little longer. The night was cool, but comfortable. Catching a glimpse of light from the corner of his eye, he turned to face it, his thumb out.

"Come on, guy. Slow down," he willed the driver.

He took a small step closer to the line marking the road, careful not to cross it. The headlights grew larger as they approached, and he was enveloped in blinding light. Covering his face with an arm, he tried to squint through the glaring lights to see the outline of the vehicle ahead. But no luck. There was a sharp squealing sound followed by a soft, dull thud, and he was sure that it was coming right for him—he wasn't far enough off the road.

Panic quickly filled him, and both arms shot up over his

face. He twisted his body so his back faced the road and squeezed his eyes shut.

Dave's momentary, and unnecessary, panic subsided as the lights hurried past him, and he was once again swallowed by darkness. Happy he hadn't just been mowed down, his heart rate still took a moment to settle. He knew his mother would be disappointed—she had a long list of reckless behaviour she didn't approve of, and hitchhiking certainly made the cut. Chuckling at the thought of his mother's constant worrying, he began to regain focus as his eyes adjusted to the darkness. Before him stood the looming outline of a large semi. He'd been so distracted by the near-miss he hadn't heard nor seen it stop.

"Hey! Thanks for stopping!" Dave shouted.

He wasn't sure if the driver could hear him at this distance. Probably not.

Then, an arm shaped shadow extended from the open window and appeared to beckon him. Dave beat feet to the truck as the outline of a person leaned from the driver's side window. Approaching the back end of the rig, out of breath, he slowed and decided to walk the rest of the way. Over the sound of his heavy breathing, he thought he heard a sound—it could have been the driver saying something, but he couldn't make it out.

The driver was an older man, maybe his dad's age. A blanket of white facial hair spread around the sides of his jawline and up to his head, which was partially covered by a dark bandana. He hung his head out the window to greet Dave with a kind and reassuring grin. Dave smiled and once again thanked the man for stopping.

"Ayah! No problem, fella! Sorry if I scared yah. These rigs ain't so easy tah loosen up once they get goin'. Name's Jerry. How 'bout you?"

"I'm David. Got a flat about two miles back."

"Some mighty bad luck, ayah."

"Tell me about it!"

"All alone out 'ere? Dark out in 'ese willie-wacks. Not very safe, yah know?"

"Yes, sir, I know. I'm ok though. I have supplies." Dave gestured to the pack he carried on his back. "Really hoping for a ride at least into the next town if possible."

The trucker's face grimaced as he reached up and scratched his right sideburn. "Climb on up! I can't leave yah out 'ere alone."

"Awesome! Thanks so much!"

Dave flanked the truck and headed to round the front end when he heard it again. Had the man said something? He turned his head curiously back in the direction of the driver. The man's gaze had shifted to inside the truck, and he was scratching his beard now. Dave was sure he heard that man say something. It seemed odd, but he shrugged it off. Probably he was just spooked from hitchhiking this empty road in the dark. The echoes of his mother's warnings didn't help either. That woman was always worried about something. The one thing Dave was sure of was that the driver hadn't been talking to him. The driver wasn't even looking at him anymore. He had heard that truckers had radios so they could talk to each other on long drives: that must have been the case here.

Dave rounded the front end of the rig and came alongside the passenger door, he grabbed hold of the door handle, then hesitated as a wave of apprehension washed over him.

He shook his head to shrug off his nervousness and pulled open the passenger door. Then, planting his foot on the step, he hoisted himself into the cab and plopped his pack on the floor in front of him. The radio in the cab was on, faintly broadcasting a news station or something to that effect. The speaker was issuing an alert about a security breach at Quantico.

That must have been what I heard, thought Dave. *Just the radio.*

Dave relaxed, laughing internally at himself for being nervous in the first place. The newscaster on the radio continued talking about a curfew issued in DC, but Jerry reached up, flipped it off, and smiled a reassuring smile.

"Don' forget yah seatbelt. Safety first in this 'ere rig," he said as he scratched his forearm.

Dave buckled up.

Jerry returned both hands to the wheel as he accelerated and steered the truck back onto the road.

Dave took a look around the inside of the truck; he had never ridden in a big rig before. It was clean enough, not like the stories he'd heard of nasty truck drivers who didn't clean out their cabs on long drives. Jerry had the classic, green, pine scented air freshener dangling from the rearview mirror, and the cab smelled just so. No lingering odours of fast food, cigarettes, or coffee. Jerry seemed to take pride in his work. Dave also noticed what appeared to be a small military clearance badge dangling from a knob on the dash.

"So, where ya headed?" Dave asked, breaking the momentary silence.

"Just made me a drop down 'ere in Virginia," Jerry said, the word sounding more like Vaginyah. "Headed back up tah Maine now. I been...scratch...takin' lobstahs down the coast fah summah."

Jerry began to scratch his scalp through the bandana, and Dave turned to look at him again. *Did he just say 'scratch'?*

Right dead in the middle of his sentence—that didn't make any sense.

Dave suddenly started to feel uncomfortable again and wasn't sure what to say. Jerry kept his eyes on the road, one hand on the wheel, and the other rubbing the back of his neck feverishly.

"Everything ok there?" Dave asked, tentatively.

"Ayah. Just got me a new soap. Got it at the truck stop back up the road apiece, an' it's upset mah skin sumthin' wicked. Been gettin' worse all day...scratch."

"Oh, man, that sucks. I guess we're both running into some bad luck today."

"Ayah, seems 'bout so."

Dave felt bad for the guy, but also started to regret this ride. He hoped the next town came sooner rather than later. Jerry was doubled over now, scratching his left leg fervently.

Man, this guy must really have an allergy or something. Come on, town. Where are you? Dave thought.

He turned his gaze out the passenger side window in an attempt to avoid the awkwardness of poor Jerry's awful itching. Leaning into the door, he laid his forehead gently against the pane of the glass window. It felt cool on his warm brow.

Suddenly, the truck swerved, and his head bounced off the glass as Jerry corrected his position on the road.

"Ow!" Dave let out a startled cry and turned his head back to the driver, lifting one hand to rub the sore spot on his forehead.

"Gaumy! This cussid itch! Lost my hands off the wheel a sec." Jerry was now scratching his face above the carpet of white beard hair. When Jerry's hands came away, Dave saw deep rivulets of blood etched into the man's face where he had been scratching. The dark liquid dripped like honey, inching its way down the man's face, and nestling into his beard, staining the white hair red.

Dave felt his stomach turn, and he suppressed the lump that started rising up into his throat: *Shit!* he thought, *this guy is fucked. Something's not right here. Where is this fucking town?*

Dave's pulse quickened. He imperceptibly scooted away from Jerry in his seat and leaned against the passenger side door a little closer, scanning the view ahead through the windshield—nothing but trees and an endless stretch of road. He didn't want to look at Jerry's blood-streaked face, but he was also afraid to turn his back on the man again. He silently begged for the next town to come into view.

Then, out of the corner of his eye, Dave saw the man's hands leave the wheel.

He turned to look at Jerry just as the truck began to swerve off the road.

"Fuck!" Dave shouted, and grabbed hold of the steering wheel, trying to correct the position of the truck.

Jerry's hands were frantically scratching—his face, his neck, his arms.

The man wrenched his bandana off his head, threw it on the dash, and began to scratch at his balding scalp, yanking and pulling on the hair that remained. Dave watched as Jerry ripped the hair from his scalp in handfuls, clumps of skin and blood still attached to the roots.

He dug divots and channels into his skin—blood oozed down his forehead, sliding through his eyebrows, and pooling into the pits of his eyes.

170

Dave thought he was going to be sick but managed a few words over his revulsion: "Hey, man! Are you ok? The truck! The tr—"

"Scratch! Scra...scra...scratch! Fucking, scratch me!" Jerry shouted as he bloodied himself and continued to tear at his skin.

Dave's eyes were locked on the man, still trying to register what was happening.

He suddenly remembered that the truck was moving forward and turned his gaze back to the road.

"Shiiiiiiit!"

Dave's hands flew up to cover his face just as the truck ran off the road and into a clump of trees with a loud, screeching crunch.

Then, full dark.

***

Dave awoke to the soft glow of light barely peeking over the horizon. A dull throb consumed his head, and his chest was on fire. He tried to look down, but a sharp, stiff pain echoed through his neck and back. His eyes found the seatbelt. The thing had saved his life, but Jesus, his chest hurt!

Jerry—Mr Put-On-Your-Seatbelt—had been ejected from his seat and was protruding half in and half out of the cab, torso propped up by the bloodied fragments of windshield that remained. Dave felt his stomach begin to curdle, but he held back the urge to vomit and shifted his gaze away from the bloodied, mangled body of the dead man.

What had happened? He could hardly remember the events that led to this. Closing his eyes, he recalled the awkwardness and the itching.

The man was itching and scratching himself, then… Jesus…did that really happen? He looked again at Jerry, and he wasn't sure. The man was a bloody mess. That clearly came from the accident, but had he been scratching? Did he scratch himself raw, or had Dave imagined that? Had Dave fallen asleep after getting in the truck?

Maybe he had dreamed the whole thing? He just wasn't sure.

Dave slowly and effortfully fumbled in his pants pocket and was able to pry out the cell phone nestled there. He ignored the notifications littering the lock screen, and dialled emergency. Carefully lifting the device to his ear, he scratched the outside of his earlobe with the top of the phone before listening for the ring.

"Hello. There's been an accident. I'm…I'm…I need some help."

Dave grimaced and let out a soft grunt as he lifted his other hand and began to scratch along his jawline. He shared his location with the dispatch, then rubbed the top of the phone back and forth against his earlobe once more.

"Yes, ma'am. I'm not going anywhere. Please hurry, I'm…"

YEAR THREE

Scratch.

Time to Say Goodbye

by D.M. Burdett

I CLOSED MY eyes against the harsh light and sucked in a deep breath through my nose. My body trembled, despite the warmth of the room.

I leaned back in the chair, my head against the wall, and tried to block out the depressing green of the relatives' room, but the clatter and noise—and the smell—still clambered for dominance over the bouncing thoughts in my head; the car, the impact, the screeching. The blood.

I exhaled a, long, slow quavering breath, trying, and failing, to steady my nerves.

Remembering an almost forgotten article about stress management, my mind went to the soles of my feet. I thought about how they felt in my shoes, where the pressure points were, and tried to relax the muscles in my legs. I emptied my mind and concentrated on my chest, feeling the tightness, the heaviness there. I breathed in deeply. I breathed out again as I counted to five. I breathed in; I breathed out. With each slow exhale, the shaking subsided, and my mind cleared.

A hand touched mine and my eyes flicked open. Nelly had joined me. My beautiful daughter. Her bright blue eyes glistened, and her wavy, blonde hair shone in the light from the window as she smiled up at me, but sadness touched the corner of her lips. She looked troubled—her cute, chubby toddler cheeks were rosy, but a confused frown furrowed her forehead. It made my heart ache. I gave her hand a light squeeze, trying to pass on a gesture of reassurance I didn't feel.

Louise let out a wail, and we both looked at her. She was curled into the chair opposite, tears rolling down her face as she sobbed, her body shuddering.

It seemed like she'd been like that for hours.

"Lou?" I breathed, but she didn't respond; deafening grief enveloped her. I reached out and gently touched her knee, but she continued to wail.

I looked back down into Nelly's face, and she looked sadder, if that were even possible. She watched her mother's pain.

Time passed.

As I listened to my wife weep, I gazed out the window that overlooked the bustling corridor. Through the dusty blinds, I watched people hurry past, going about their business as if nothing had happened. As if this wasn't the worst day.

The last day.

Time seemed to stand still and rush by, all at once.

Nelly lay her head in my lap, and I pushed my fingers

through her hair, feeling the silkiness, the softness. She closed her eyes and soon her breathing became slow and steady, the sadness melting from her cherubic face. It made me smile; a moment of calm in the madness.

I felt drained, exhausted. Useless. Lou's crying was tearing at my heart. She was inconsolable, but there was nothing I could do to help her. Nothing I could say.

I let her grieve as Nelly slept in my lap.

After a time that seemed endless, a nurse entered the room and kneeled in front of Lou, putting a hand on her arm.

"Are you ready to come through?" the nurse asked, kindly, patiently, and Louise rose slowly, her legs quivering.

It was time to say goodbye.

I gave Nelly a gentle shake and she looked up at me with bleary eyes, stretching her arms out.

I was tired too, and my own eyes felt so heavy. "Come on, Pumpkin," I said wearily.

At the sound of my voice, Louise glanced over at me, her brow furrowed. I thought she might speak then, the first words since the accident, but after only a moment's pause, her eyes dropped to the floor, and she followed the nurse from the room.

We walked down grey corridors, Nelly's tiny hand in mine, passing strangers who didn't give us a second glance. I marvelled at how everything could be so normal for them. How could they be smiling, laughing? Their nonchalance angered me. Nelly wiggled her fingers and frowned up at me, and I realised how tightly I was gripping her hand.

"Sorry, Pumpkin," I said with a smile. Louise looked over her shoulder at us.

I wondered if she blamed me for the accident. Or maybe she blamed herself.

But it no longer mattered.

We stopped outside another room; the blinds closed. The nurse turned and touched Lou's arm before pushing open the door, holding it open as she ushered her inside.

Nelly and I followed but waited by the door.

Lou stumbled when she saw the twin beds, side by side, and I reached out instinctively, but the nurse was already there, holding Lou's arm and steering her to the chair between the two beds. Lou slumped into it, her face in her hands, not wanting to look.

She lowered her hands and screamed.

My heart tore in two, and Nelly wrapped her arms around my leg, her cheek pressed against my thigh. A single tear traced a path down her rosy cheek.

We watched from the doorway as my wife reached out, her hands shaking, and grasped the hands of her dead daughter and husband.

"Goodbye, Mumma," Nelly whispered as we left.

The Body Truck

by Jason Hardy

WE FIND ONE slumped against a mailbox on Barrow, hand probing the machete notched broadside his skull. He brightens when he sees us; thinks we're here to help. Larson helps him, alright…with a spike through the eye. We heave the body onto the truck.

On Flagler, we spot a lady in a creepy doll getup, gut-shot and groaning. She sees our uniforms and understands. Even tries to crawl away. Carney does the honours.

City's always a bloody mess after the big night. Cleaning gigs pay well. Job's simple: put the bodies on the truck.

Including the ones still breathing.

Recon

by Andrew McDonald

THE SENTRY NEVER heard me. I stab all the way through his neck, behind the jugular. Pushing the blade forward, I tear out his throat. He dies without even a whisper. Quietly, I drag him into the woods, away from patrols.

With my hatchet, I split his skull, careful not to harm the brain. My knife severs the brainstem. Raising the brain to my lips, I sink my teeth into it, biting off gory chunks, swallowing the grey matter.

Closing my eyes, I sift through his memories. Childhood, first love, basic training, their hidden headquarters.

I radio for an airstrike.

Sacrifice

by Darlene Holt

AFTER ALIENS INVADED, war waged against humanity, and civilians sacrificed normalcy to join the cause. Command assured us training wasn't necessary, despite our lack of military experience. Just an injection to ward off illness.

When they released us into the streets to kill the invaders, I hid, paralysed by fear, as eight-foot, razor-toothed creatures devoured anyone crossing their paths. To my surprise, the aliens fell dead on the blood-splattered asphalt minutes after swallowing my human comrades.

Only then did I realise Command had injected us with a toxin. They didn't need to train us after all; they only needed bait.

Phoenix Fighters

by Dawn DeBraal

THOUSANDS OF THEM, dead. Commander Helmet observed ravaged bodies as far as his eyes could see. Total devastation. His exhausted men sat, welcoming the reprieve while fresh recruits took up the grave detail. The men dug trenches, throwing dead bodies into them, while great fires rose, hot enough to burn the corpses.

A scream in the night. Helmet mounted his steed, riding out onto the battlefield. Even though his men had annihilated the enemy, the dead were coming back to life.

Soldiers screamed, running off. Mesmerised, Helmet watched the jerky movements of the newly risen, willing to  do battle again.

Abraham and Isaac

by James Rumpel

"DADDY, CAN I have a gun?" asked little Isaac. "I can shoot the monsters just as well as Jimmy."

"I'm sure you could, son. But you have a much more important job to do. The government says this is the best way to defeat the invaders. We have to slow them down. Otherwise, they are too fast, and we wouldn't have time to get our shots off."

"Okay, but I want a gun next time."

Abraham smiled, though he felt no joy. "Sure, you can have a gun next time. Now, go sit on the rock and close your eyes."

Private Edad

by John Lane

BEFORE THE COMMENCEMENT of Operation Overlord, the newest soldier of First Infantry Division composed a letter, an effort to reassure his mother. She feared losing him to a bullet like her father during the Great War.

In writing, Private Joseph Edad promised to see her again.

Then, on D-Day, as he marched up Omaha Beach, several rounds of ammo from a German's MG-42 drilled into his neck. The soldier was the first to fall.

For his last seconds of life, he never thought about his fellow soldiers silencing the German gunners.

He only hoped he didn't make his mother angry.

183

My Body

by Marion Lougheed

I FLOAT ABOVE the body that used to be mine, imagining I will break free if only I tug hard enough. Our corpses blanket the field, our blood already drying. Our enemy has slain us all.

"Help me!" I call, but I am voiceless. The survivors straggle up the hill. A chill replaces the heat of battle.

An enemy soldier passes close enough for me to touch with my ghostly fingers. He shivers and a spasm shoots through him. He falls. My ethereal grip sinks into his warmth, then I am pushing his essence aside.

This body is mine now.

Battle of the Bands

by N.E. Rule

O N HER PATIO, Linda's jaw clenches in determination as she starts her classical music. Exactly one minute later, punk rock blasts back at her from her enemy's yard.

She storms onto his deck. His words strike first from his hot tub. "Dumb bitch, stealing my batteries is the best you got? Here's a shocker, I got a cord." He nods to the boombox plugged into an exterior outlet.

Linda smiles. "I hoped so. Here's another shocker." She tips the boombox into the water. His music stops dead. Wide eyes slip below the surface as Tchaikovsky's "1812 Overture" hits a crescendo.

Dual

by Pauline Yates

WHY'D YOU BRING me home, Jimmy? Couldn't hack a third tour of duty? The war ain't over. You and me, we make the best team. But you're a coward, ain't ya, Jimmy? Shit, if it wasn't for me, you'd be rotting in a body bag.

Is this how you repay me? Drag me into fucking therapy, get drugs to stop our nightmares? I don't want them to stop. They keep us wired and fired, Jimmy. Wired and fired. Get that into your chicken head.

The war ain't over, Jimmy. It will never be over. Not while I'm in your head.

This Means War

by Wednesday Paige

I CAN'T REMEMBER a time when it wasn't like this—the *why* has evaporated into ancient history.

"Cheeky fuckers!" Rick had exclaimed after receiving their note: "You were loud last night. 'I'm coming!' 3 times (yeah, right)."

I thought he'd be satisfied with knocking copper nails into their precious trees…until one fell onto our garage.

They're not so innocent either: sneaking into our garden to steal our chickens; taking our post; filling our dustbin after it's been emptied.

I can't help thinking it's gone too far as he pulls their bulging-eyed chihuahua—its tongue hanging out—from our freezer.

Deserts of Blood

by Leanbh Pearson

UNDER THE DESERT sun, the sand is clotted with scarlet gore; the blood of the vanquished. The lion-headed goddess roars in her bloodlust, the golden light of Ra upon his vengeful daughter.

"Sekhmet!"

The armies of Egypt fall to their knees to appease her, offering up prayers in her name. These warriors in blood-stained armour, armed with blades that slice and hack, these men who scream and die. This battlefield is her dominion, her temple—her feast. But still she hungers, prowling the battleground, fangs exposed, bloody sickles at her side. And until, Sekhmet is satiated, war will rage.

The Great Sacrifice

by Joel R. Hunt

ADMIRAL TIROSH WATCHED ten thousand uniformed men and women march into the portal, rifles at the ready, faces determined. They thought they knew what they would face on the other side, but they were wrong.

None would return.

As the portal closed, Tirosh's holopad lit up with the face of his enemy.

"We demand more meat," said the alien.

"More?" replied Tirosh. "We can't keep sacrificing our people like this."

The alien laughed.

"Your humans are happy believing in this pretend war against us. What difference does it make if their children die on the battlefield or the buffet table?"

Thank You for Your Service

by Steven Lord

THE CROSSHAIRS REST *just above the target's spine.*

Cold zero.

That's what we call these shots. No chance to learn the pull of the rifling, or the lie of the scope.

The flag flutters slightly in the wind. I adjust my aim half a degree left.

I've scored seven kills this way in Afghan. A lifetime of war, Medal of Honour to show for it.

I exhale halfway out, gently squeeze the trigger.

You thanked me for my service, then sent me out again. And again. No more.

I turn and walk away as the crowd's cheers turn to screams.

The Skittering

by Stephen Herczeg

INSECTS. AFTER DECADES of Hollywood telling us that aliens were little green men, they finally arrived. And they were insects. Bigger than rhinos. Tougher than cockroaches. And hungry.

The first wave hit New York. Ripping apart people like they were dolls. We deployed within hours. Thousands swarmed the streets; the sound of skittering feet was everywhere. Filling my mind.

Regular bullets were no good, only armour piercing rounds.

Suddenly, the skittering stopped. They disappeared. Leaving only silence.

And waiting. For hours.

Then the skittering started again.

I see one. Fire. Nothing.

The bullets don't work. They've changed.

God save us.

The Fog of War

by Warren Benedetto

JAMESON SURVEYED THE battle-scarred landscape. Shadows rose from the mud, moving through the fog obscuring the carnage. The sharp smell of cordite hung in the air. Jameson's ears were numb—the only sound was the agonising wail of an injured soldier on the ground beneath him. Shrapnel had shredded the man's face; his stomach was a gurgling pile of entrails. Jameson read the patch on the man's blood-soaked uniform. The name was familiar: T. Jameson.

His own.

Damn it, Jameson thought, recalling the whistling of the incoming mortar. *Direct hit.*

He sighed, then joined the other shadows in the fog.

Was It Plato?

by Avery Hunter

C AKED IN NO-MAN'S-LAND mud, ears still ringing from the explosion that took my leg—I haven't yet realised its gone, there's just a dull throb where it used to be—I blink shit from my eyes.

Jimmy lies next to me, a smile on his face. "It's over, Lance," he says, clear as day. "Isn't the end of war beautiful?"

A mortar lands close by. We get showered in dirt again. "What're ya talking about, Jimmy?"

I look over. He's long gone; his brains are seeping into the mud.

"Only the dead have seen the end of war," he whispers.

The Truth About Lisa

by Karen Bayly

LISA SMOOTHED HER long hair, admiring its gentle russet waves. Her fingers strayed to the strands framing her face. Gently, she pulled these in front of her eyes, searching for telltale drops of blood. Ah, there was one. Ruby red and still glistening. She licked it away, relishing its tang. Never waste a morsel. Wasn't that what Francesco had taught her?

As her creator and husband, it was only right he should teach her to conduct herself appropriately. The etiquette of feasting, the subterfuge of the damned—these were lessons essential to her survival. She could not rely on him forever. His age meant he would leave this life before she did. There might be many years alone before she also departed her privileged existence here.

Of course, neither of them would die. Their kind lived for centuries. But to remain in one location for too long invited trouble. Best fake one's demise at a suitable age, then move to another country, learn a new language, begin again.

Lifting her skirts, she stepped over the bloodied and mangled body at her feet. The young woman had been delicious, but oh so filling. Neither she nor her husband would require more food for days now, an advantage of being a cold-blooded predator. Fortuitously, peasants had disappeared from the streets of Florence for as long as she remembered. Nonetheless, Francesco had instilled in her the need for prudence. No point in drawing undesirable attention to oneself.

Overall, the poor might be unknown and unwanted, but they provided her with what she needed. Young folk, male or female, ripe for sport, fornication, feasting. With her nose, she could sniff out the spicy aroma of their hormones, hidden under the pungent sweat of their bodies.

How she adored the looks on their faces as she lured them into her carriage—amazement, unworthiness, and desire, all at once! They were filthy with dirt and bodily secretions, but it was nothing a perfumed kerchief over one's nose couldn't remedy.

Anyway, once home, she insisted they bathe before they entered her chamber. Some complained, convinced bathing in scented waters was sinful, but the promise of food, wine, pleasure, and money always won.

She smiled. Maybe baths were the devil's work, leading them straight to hell. At the very least, the fragrant water made a marinade to sweeten their meat. And such flesh! Ripe with worldly lusts, easy to tempt into sin, and easier to savour. A frisson of delight ran up her spine.

Francesco popped his head into the room.

"Lisa, *amore mio*. The painter is here."

He glanced at the body on the floor.

"I'll get Antonio to clean that up. There's enough for him to chew on, and plenty of bones for cook's soup."

"*Grazie*, Francesco."

She curtsied graciously and hurried out the door. She'd been lucky to marry so well. Her husband may have ensured her exclusion from heaven, but he was kind and attentive. So charming of him to commission a portrait with such a renowned artist. She hastened upstairs to the sitting room.

Sunlight streamed in through the open window, casting a golden glow over the dark wood furniture and lush furnishings. On one wall hung rich tapestries depicting hunting scenes and ancient castles. Opposite stood the painter behind his easel.

"Ah, La Gioconda," said Leonardo. "You look radiant this morning."

His flattery tickled her, yet she stifled her laughter.

"No smile?"

The remnants of her bloodlust lingered, and her teeth remained as pointy and sharp as tiny knives. Best to restrict herself to enigmatic grins.

Ever the modest wife, she bowed her head as she answered.

"Not today, da Vinci. A little elusiveness suits a woman, *sì*?"

She swept over to the chair and settled into an elegant pose, letting her right arm rest on her full, digesting belly.

Leonardo nodded in appreciation.

"Your mystery will be ageless, *bella*."

The corners of her mouth dimpled as she teased him with a sideways glance. Her mystery was best left unknown.

Yanking The Devil's Chain

by A.H. Syme

ON'T TELL ME you can't feel that gaping hole inside your body. I cannot abide lies, and I shall rip out your tongue," the demon said, flashing his sharp teeth.

I hesitated. I really couldn't feel any such thing. The sulphur smell in this place made me feel sick, as did the decorative panels of upside-down crucified figures. They moaned softly, and frankly, some of them stunk. Talk about art imitating life.

He'd got that down pat.

Look, I know this is a shock to you, but I don't intend to follow you any more through this dark, rocky cavern. It's hot down here, and the further we go, the more uncomfortable my feet get with the heat," I said, trying not to sound petulant.

He stopped, turned quickly and sent his long arrow-shaped tail whipping around behind him. He glared down at my sneakers, his top lip curling.

I didn't like it. "Hey, they are the best I could afford," I said defensively

"What on earth is that?" he said, pointing a bony, clawed finger at the pattern on my shoes.

"They're pirate skull-and-crossbones," I said, not embarrassed by them in the least.

"See there," he aimed the same bony finger over to a boulder where I could make out naked figures of males and females chained to the rock's side. Sweat ran down their flesh, and their hair hung in lank strands around their heads. They had one of their sandshoes in flames on their feet. Curling and bubbling their skin, their eyes wide with pain, but unable to scream because the other sandshoe was rammed in their mouths. I noticed the shoes were all tartan. This dude certainly didn't like Scots.

"That's what happens to things I don't like," he said.

His foul breath washing over me like rotten meat. I thought about suggesting some kind of mouth wash or a peppermint maybe, but a fluorescent-pink sandshoe caught my attention.

"Why's that one different?" I asked.

"I don't like the colour," he said, whipping back around again.

"I guess the sole of shame isn't for me," I said, smiling at my wit.

"No. I have something better planned. I know you think you are hallucinating this whole thing, but look," he said pointing that bony claw again.

On top of a platform carved from the rock's face, a pack of dogs with female heads wailed and howled. I couldn't see how they had got up there, nor how they could get down. They circled and paced round and round continuously over their small rocky domain. I noticed they avoided doing the usual doggie greeting thing, but some did scratch, and others squatted to pee.

"Wow," I said. "That's some stuck up bitches."

He ignored me and pointed again.

I could see a group of naked men getting chunks bitten out of their legs and arms; some had their stomachs and thighs bitten, others were missing their penises. They seemed unable to ward off the attacks by a horde of sickly, obese looking creatures with huge eyes and smaller mouths.

"That's awful. Why are they greedily biting like that?" I asked,

"They're eating McDonalds," he said.

"Look, man, if you have some sort of Celt hate thing going on, I'm not Scottish," I said.

"I know," he said, walking on through the dull, reddish light that did little to illuminate this dark underground cave.

I was compelled against my will to follow. We passed through an area where, at first, I thought it was stalactites hanging from the ceiling. Then I realised by the ooze on the ground that it was people, their putrefied inners dripping down to puddle beneath them.

"That is totally gross," I said. "It's disgusting."

"Now, now," the horned beast with pus-filled, scaly skin said. "Don't be like that. Each to our own. You like your popsicles; I like my corpsicles."

He laughed then, for the first time, a horrible noise of high grating squeals that reverberated and thumped off the rock walls. I covered my ears; it sounded terrible, like being stuck in a Bay City Rollers concert. I didn't know what I disliked the most, the sound or the fact that I may have picked up the anti-Scots bug.

"And where is all the sex? I haven't seen one orgy," I asked.

The demon seemed confused or surprised; I was unsure which expression I was looking at with him having such an ugly face.

"You know, humping; screwing; rumpy-pumping; doing it; hanky-panky; porking. Shagging, doing squat thrusts in the cucumber patch; the beast with two backs; buttering a biscuit. I have to tell you, I'm really, really disappointed."

"Squats in a cucumber patch! The beast with two backs! Buttering a biscuit! Sex! Don't be so revolting. That's absolutely horrendously disgusting. There is none of that awful bonking here," the demon yelled, turning his back and hurrying on.

I had been wrong; it wasn't bewilderment that had been on his face, it had been shock.

Further along, a giant, black spider stretched out wide, its eight legs across the centre of its web. In its palps, it held a baby, and it sunk its fangs into the tender flesh, injecting the small, thrashing being with digestive fluid, which rapidly liquefied the inside of the body. I noticed many more babies stuck along each glistening thread. And fine, pink-skinned exoskeletons—discarded human husks—littering the floor below the giant web.

"Oh, come on now," I said. "Since when are babies evil? You can't be doing this," I protested.

He stopped in front of the suspended monstrosity, his cloven feet crushing and rustling the hollow skins. "Don't be a fool. Of course, I can't take babies. These are mature adults shrunk down into this miniature baby size," he said, glaring at me. "And be careful what you say; I don't want certain unwanted ramifications. And if that happens, you will suffer worse than all the souls in hell."

I shrugged. "I once had to listen to 'Achy Breaky Heart', ten times straight, and still didn't get laid. So do your worse, kiddo," I said, glancing up at the spider. "Ah, now I get it. It's on a reduced diet," I said.

He started to snort smoke out of his nostrils. "Your humour will not save you down here," he said, stomping his cloven hoof on the ground. I noticed it sent rats with gaping mouths scurrying into any cracks they could find. And I do mean any cracks. I felt myself tightening my butt cheeks.

"Okay," I said. "Let's just say it likes jelly babies."

He snorted flames of rage out through his nostrils; they shot upwards, igniting some other gases in the malodorous air. A few bats with human feet screeched as they tried to avoid the flames.

"It's a shame you don't drink sambucas; that trick would come in handy," I said.

It was too much for the evil creature. It lurched forward and grabbed me by the throat.

I could clearly see its reptilian pupils—slits, black, deep and ominous, in a being without any light. The irises of the beast were crimson with blood that leaked and stained the scales under its eye sockets. Its breath was beyond putrid. I felt my nostril hair shrivel.

"Here's your place, now," he said, lifting me by the neck and putting me down in front of a lake filled with faeces. He released me.

I coughed and spluttered. In front of me, at least a thousand people stood up to their waists in shit. "You have got to be joking," I said. "I heard a joke like this once and—" My voice was cut off by a siren's loud, droning sound. I watched in horror as the people dipped their heads under the sea of foul, brown, stinking matter, and their legs appeared in the air.

"Now, don't say I don't have a sense of humour," the Devil said.

I couldn't say anything; I was mortified. The demon pointed its finger for me to get in. I squeezed my eyes shut and said, "Dear Lord…"

It was all it took for a blinding flash of light to appear. I could see it through my closed lids; the brightness was amazing. I opened my eyes, and an Archangel of the Lord stood there. He was powerful and glorious with massive, white wings as pure as new snow spread out wide behind his back. His face was classically handsome, his torso bare and ripped. Around his hips, hanging suggestively low, was draped a white loincloth. He stood with his feet apart, and in front of his body, he held in both hands, a huge sword, its tip touching the ground, causing roses to grow.

"Oh, now you've done it. He's here," the Devil spat his contempt. "And stop holding that ridiculous sword like an enlarged phallic symbol between your legs. It's so boringly tedious, Michael," he snapped.

"Oh, I don't know," I said, wrapping my arms around Michael's mighty arm. "I rather like it."

The air shimmered, and I felt myself rapidly moving upwards. I could hear the dreadful demon spewing his raging hate towards us, but in a flash, we were gone.

I brushed myself off, and Michael waved his hand, transforming me back to myself.

"And they think I'm the devil," I said, putting out my hand. "Come on, you promised me the horn of Cornucopia for a couple of days," I said.

"Man," Michael said. "I do love it when you wind that dude up. Thanks, Pan," he said, giving me the horn and my flute.

"The next time I'm down there, remind me to bring an enormous bag of peppermints and to wear tighter underwear. Just in case," I said, with a wink, and using my

YEAR THREE

own cloven hoofs and nimble goat legs, I quickly disappeared.

The Gauntlet

by April Yates

I RECKON THESE girls will make it across easy."

The line crackled across the hundred miles separating the two gas stations.

"You say that every time."

'Nah, I'm right this time, they're together, I think. One of 'em has a real hard look in her eyes; she's been through some shit, that'll help."

The road between has many tricks and illusions.

A woman and small child broken down in need of help, an injured dear; all seemingly innocuous and designed to lure you out of the safety of your car.

All designed to kill you, if you're lucky that is.

The Näcken's Music

by Leanbh Pearson

THE MUSICIAN SAT beside the hearth, clothing threadbare and hair unkempt.

"Don't ask me to play. I cannot resist."

Men laughed, eyeing the wretch. "You something special then?"

He lifted the battered fiddle. "A Näcken was drowning children in a brook. If I answered his three questions, he'd gift this instrument and his uncanny music to me. And I bested him but cursed myself."

"Play for us then," someone scoffed.

Smiling wearily, he obliged. The music was as sweet as a midsummer brook, gentle like raindrops on a lake, but it dragged us under to our graves all the same.

Sea Food

by Birgit K. Gaiser

THE BODY SINKS noiselessly, slowly, its density just exceeding that of its salty grave.

We patiently wait while the water softens the skin. Our army of custodians watches, approaches. Crabs and shrimp kiss cold lips, gently gnawing, pinching. When the skin breaks, squat lobsters join in to feed on blood, fat and muscle. A shark perturbs the peaceful banquet, chomping chunks out of the body, ripping through fabric and bones.

A foot escapes before we can finish our meal. Lifted by the shoe's air pockets, it floats upwards, sunwards, to wash up on a beach and re-join its own kind.

Stranger Danger

by Pauline Yates

I DON'T LIKE this murky underwater playground. The other girls leer at me with toothy grins, mocking my ignorance. You were warned, they say, their silent whispers escaping like milkshake bubbles through rotting nasal cavities. I was. But not my friend, Chelsey—she was the first.

She's at the edge of the group, her bloated body held down by a rope tied to a rock. He wasn't as careful with me. My ankle rope is loose. After the crabs feast on my flesh, I'll slip free and drift to the lake's surface. I'll help catch our killer. By being found.

Facade

by Jo Mularczyk

LOOK MAMA, A mermaid!" The child's shriek of wonder froze on her lips as the creature turned from its perch upon the rock.

The golden tendrils the child had admired were revealed to be a web of sand-infested kelp writhing with tortured sea urchins. The creature's skin was a pallid green, rent by a wretched scar that stretched across one cheek. Blood-red eyes emitted a foul stream that ran down the foetid cheeks and dripped into the water below.

The creature twisted its mouth into a depraved rictus that would haunt the child eternally, before diving elegantly beneath the waves.

Little Brother

by Fiona M. Jones

THE BAD DREAMS started when he was a baby. He got eaten by wild animals, struck by lightning, he fell from terrible heights or drowned in deep water… and every time I am paralysed, unable to save him.

I would wake, sweating, silently screaming, and slowly breathe again.

The day he fell off the harbour wall, I froze—as usual—in a silent scream and waited to wake up again.

"Why didn't you HELP him?" they asked afterwards. But my nightmares have stopped. Now in my dreams he is there under the water, laughing, waiting for me to join him.

Clearest Waters

by Jake Jerome

THE TRAVEL BROCHURE said these are the clearest waters in the world, and God, it's true. I can see everything. The coral reefs. The fish whose species I'll never know. The hermit crab taking residence inside of my hollowed out foot.

I didn't lose much blood when Mr Hermit came along and picked away the flesh piecemeal. These rocks I slipped on have a vice grip on my ankle. Snapped the fibula and closed the arteries.

Every movement under the metatarsal cage looks like a fluttering heart.

He's got the best shell in town.

And I have the worst view.

Loophole

by Brian Maycock

BRAIN DAMAGE BEGINS after three minutes.

He admired the perfect blue sea. Submerged. Mouth clamped closed.

Eight minutes is all it can take for death to occur.

That would not be him.

He had always been a risk taker. Now he was a killer with a lot to live for.

The insurance pay out from his wife's death was in the millions and appeared spent, but most was fractured into untraceable digital nest eggs.

So what if the police were closing in.

He watched his watch tick past three minutes.

It was time to emerge, not fit to stand trial.

Bait

by Constantine E. Kiousis

TINA SWAM TOWARDS the bluish glow—around her nothing but dark, cold water. Her mind in a fog, she tried to remember how she'd found herself here, but could only grasp at bits and pieces.

She recalled boating a bit off the coast for a nightly scuba-dive. She remembered gearing up and dropping back-first into the black ocean.

Then nothing.

But she didn't really care.

All that mattered was the light, drawing her like a moth to a flame.

She barely had time to notice the huge opaque eyes hidden behind it, above a gaping maw of elongated, pointy teeth.

The Blue Cage

by Patrick Shanley

SHE COULD STILL hear the mournful calls of her kingdom, echoing through that grand, blue cathedral as the soft, pink hands of her captors ripped her from its halls. They cried for her, drifting away into blackness as the land-apes hauled her onto their floating shell and took her far away.

Every night she heard them, flooding back to her as she idled in this cramped tank, weary from a day of entertaining the harping land-apes, fat, cruel and doughy.

She would make them know she was a queen. Soon.

She would remind them why they called her kind killers.

Catch and Release

by Robyn Fraser

SUNRISE, AND A misty river. Three trout, hooked and thrown back. He preferred to fish humanely.

Something glittered in the reeds. He reached for it, and metal teeth clamped over his fingers. A line tautened and pulled him into the water, screaming and thrashing.

It felt like an eternity under there. His lungs were bursting, eyes bulging from his head. It seemed—*but impossible!*—something huge was holding him, measuring him, ripping the trap off his hand, and two fingers along with it.

He was flung up onto the rocks, vomiting water and fighting for air.

Caught.

And released.

Humanely.

The Waiting Game

by S.L. Kretschmer

I LIE PROSTRATE on the ocean floor, clutching the scuba tank to my chest. Silence, except for the exaggerated echo of my breaths. Shafts of hazy, muted sunlight edge tantalisingly close to my supine body. It can't be more than eight metres to the surface.

Clownfish dart to my left, disappearing into the coral. A seahorse bucks and rears in the ocean current. I check the gauge. My air is running out; soon I won't have a choice.

The great fish returns, languidly gliding above me. It's shadow inches along my body, sending a shiver down my spine.

Not yet.

Fishing with Frankie

by Caoimhin Kennedy

I BAIT THE hook and toss my line.

Pluksh! goes the sinker.

I look down at my feet into my bucket full of fish. They're really biting tonight. In fact…

Yep!

I crank the reel. *Look at that—another one!*

I drop the fish into the bucket and re-apply the hearty bait to my hook.

I think of how that bastard Frankie said I would never catch anything in these waters.

I toss my line.

"Useless pig," I mutter to myself, still thinking of Frankie.

I realise quickly that statement's a lie. He's pretty darn useful as bait.

Treasured

by Kimberly Rei

THE CRYSTAL RIVER lives up to its name. Every year, tourists flock to gaze into clear waters, to admire herds of manatee, to kayak on lazy summer days.

Lila watched from her favourite hiding spot.

They called the gentle river giants "mermaids," and they were treasured. But there were always a few who couldn't resist tormenting and harming.

Lila heard crude laughter. Two idiot boys leaned over a canoe, jabbing at a manatee with oars.

Another splash and both were gone. Shadowy mermaids swam back down to less clear depths, human bodies in tow.

The manatee were treasured. And protected.

Salt

by Rachel R.

THE AIR IS bracing wet and winter cold. The sun beats down, relentless, but below, at the bone white bar, the men shiver into their cups.

A grizzled old sea dog shakes his head, cackling in the corner.

"That one's gone salt mad," a younger man whispers to his bespectacled companion. "Saw his whole crew leap into the blue, screaming about sharp toothed sea-women."

"Patently ridiculous," says the bespectacled man, shaking his head.

"Quite," says the younger man.

Pointed teeth flash in the dim light. "They weren't all women."

The salt-mad man laughs.

Then, a smile, a scream, and silence.

Surfacing

by Matt Krizan

KARINA LINGERS AT the end of the dock, watching for Ryan to resurface. The water shimmers in the moonlight, while cicadas drown out the sound of gentle waves lapping against the pilings. She shuts her eyes as she remembers their early days together, skinny-dipping on summer nights just like this one.

Five minutes of waiting becomes ten, then a half-hour—still no sign of Ryan.

A warm breeze tugs loose the scarf concealing the mark of his hands around her throat. Karina sighs, tension seeps from her neck and shoulders.

She'd been afraid she hadn't weighed his body down enough.

The Cupboard Under the Stairs

by Karen Bayly

THE LAST HIGH note of Emmy's ballad hung in the air as the crowd rose, filling the auditorium with tumultuous applause. She bowed and blew kisses to her adoring fans. From stage left, an old lady entered carrying an armful of lilies. The budding star opened her arms to receive the bouquet, but the woman tossed the blooms on the bed, where they turned into a pile of clean washing.

"Emmy, for chrissakes! I warned you. I've had enough of your squallin'."

"Ain't squallin', Gran. Singin'."

Without another word, Granny grabbed her skinny granddaughter in a headlock and yanked her down the stairs. The young girl protested, putting up as much resistance as her grandmother's iron hold would allow. Years of working the land had made the old woman hard.

"Don't care. You're drivin' me nuts. And quit wrigglin' like a worm." She threw open the door to the cupboard at the bottom of the stairs. "In with you."

Emmy landed unceremoniously in a heap amidst old toys and empty boxes. The space stank of rat piss and dead things. An ancient bobblehead stared at her from a shelf, shaking its head in dismay, admonishing, You've been a bad girl.

The light reduced to a thin sliver, peeking through a gap under the door. A rustling in the corner sent a shiver down her spine. She scuttled away from the source and rattled the lock.

"Gran, let me out! I'll be good."

"Darn it, girl. I said shut it! You'll get let out when I'm good an' ready."

The sound of her grandmother's footsteps stomping upstairs dampened the last flame of rebellion in Em's soul. Defeated, she wrapped her bare arms around her bony knees and whimpered.

The rustling grew louder. As she struggled to focus in the gloom, she shifted her body, hoping what little light existed was enough to illuminate the source of the noise. Not a chance. The far wall of the cupboard appeared to stretch into infinity.

Now the sound came from the two side walls. Em thought she saw the beady eyes of rats, hungry and cruel. Rats terrified her. Gran knew that.

Something nibbled her toe where the flesh peeked out from her sandals.

An almighty scream erupted from her body, tearing through the air to the rooms above.

Footsteps thundered down the stairs.

"What in God's name is the matter with you, girl?"

"The rats, Gran! The rats are eating me!"

"Oh, for chrissakes! Do I have to whip you to shut—"

The rhythm of Gran's descent broke as though her feet were taking a breath, the temporary silence punctuated by a cry of despair and a loud thump.

No more sliver of light.

"Gran?"

A soft moan, a single note answer, then nothing.

"Gran!?"

Em wiggled her fingers under the door and prodded the warm solid flesh of her grandmother lying on the floor, blocking the exit.

"Wake up!"

Gran didn't move.

The rustling began again. Louder, and from all over the room.

Em leapt up, let out a banshee war cry, and kicked like a mule, sending boxes flying, scattering toys. She jumped up and down, hoping to crush the wretched vermin beneath her feet. A loud squeak sounded from under her right foot, and she backed away, sliding down the wall until her butt hit the ground.

Had she just squished a rat? Or only a toy?

She ran her hand over her sandal. The sole was dry and dusty, but maybe she hadn't stamped on the critter hard enough to break it open. Or kill the varmint. What if she'd merely injured the beast? The poor thing could be dying slowly and in agony. Even though she hated rats, the notion of any animal suffering made her sick to her gut.

Taking off her sandal, she poked around where she thought the rat or toy might be. Nothing. She prodded left, then right. Still nothing. Perhaps she imagined the squeak.

Anyway, the rustling had stopped.

She pushed her fingers under the door again. Gran lay there, not making a sound. Em couldn't tell if she was breathing.

"Gran? Please wake up. I won't sing no more."

No response.

Tears streamed down Em's face. If Gran didn't wake, who would save her? Her brother, Joe, was working two shifts at the factory and wouldn't be home until 10:00 pm. That was at least twelve hours away.

She closed her eyelids, willing herself to stay calm. If the rustling didn't start again, she'd be okay.

A firm, wet tongue licked her face. Both her eyelids shot open, but her body froze in terror.

Then it spoke, a single baritone squeak in her left ear. Her eyes swivelled, trying to see what lurked in the dark. Beside her stood a giant rat, its fur musty with the odour of decay. A paw the size of a toddler's hand clamped down on her shoulder.

From around the room, a chorale of squeaks arose to welcome their king. The number of singers grew with every stanza, coalescing into a cacophony of exultation.

Its breath was on her face now. She opened her mouth to scream, but no sound came out. Her limbs refused to obey any command.

Sharp incisors bit into her cheek and gnawed, biting through muscle and crunching bone. The chorale crescendoed, accompanied by a percussion of rustling as the rats surged toward her, ravening, desperate to rip into her flesh.

Emmy's screams finally loosed into an aria of pain.

Outside, her grandmother stirred, semi-conscious.

"Chrissakes, girl, stop your squallin'."

A rivulet of blood trickled toward the old woman's face. Her gaze followed its progress, her eyes slowly clouding over. She smiled, hearing her granddaughter had slipped into silence. Peace at last.

The Feast of the Taliban Spiders

by Mike Rader

I LOOKED ACROSS the hovel to where the Taliban had tied their victims to slabs. Three men—one young, two old—lay naked and lashed at the wrists and ankles with taut leather cords.

The youngest died in a frenzy of hideous screams. From where I was, I couldn't see what they had done to him. The man next to him, much older, had been screaming too, then suddenly stopped. Maybe a merciful heart attack had saved him from further agony.

The man nearest me was still alive, and my eyes were riveted on him. He bucked against his restraints, arching his back, whimpering. His breathing was accelerated. I could only imagine his absolute fear.

His skin had the texture of old paper, yellowed with age, his ancient nipples slack. The veins on his neck were as rigid as rope as the first spiders crawled over his feet.

Spiders...*so that was the Taliban's method of torture...*

I watched them carefully. The spiders were various sizes, the bigger ones lumbering along grimly, the smaller ones moving in short, agitated leaps and bursts, darting over the wizened flesh.

Soon spiders were swarming up the old man's legs.

climbing over his scaly knees, exploring the black wiry thatch of his groin. His worn face was streaked with sweat.

I wondered when it would be my turn...

They say spiders could eat every human on earth. The world's spiders devour something like 800 million tons of prey a year. Spiders eat more meat than all seven billion humans do. In fact, the total weight of all humanity—about 350 million tons—would be a nice snack for spiders. Which, personally, I find fascinating.

I saw the tarantulas were on the move. Black, hairy, sinister; they were a marvel to see. Some were gigantic, some as wide as a human hand, others as big as a dinner plates. I knew a lot about them; named after Taranto in Italy, they were smart and made their own silk to line their burrows, stabilising the walls and making it easier to climb in and out. Their hollow fangs were located just below their eyes and directly forward of their mouths, so they can shoot venom any which way. Real smart killing machines.

I studied their progress up the old man's body, the way they explored his navel, circled his nipples, and proceeded up to his neck.

The old man's face was a surging mass of black terror. He opened his mouth to scream. Mistake! I watched spiders disappear onto his tongue between his teeth and burrow up his nostrils, and I could imagine the turmoil in his brain.

And then—

At last—

YEAR THREE

Inevitably—

It was my turn.

The Taliban are very clever. They'd brought me in, safely caged, from the jungle. Me, the Goliath bird-eating spider, with a similar biomass of what you humans call a puppy. My legs are twelve inches long, and my body alone is the size of a large human fist, *a very large human fist.*

My cage door was whipped open.

I think the old man heard my approach. My sharp, hard claws made a clicking sound on the slab. His eyes widened.

The other spiders saw me coming and bolted. Some didn't move fast enough. I rubbed my hind legs against my abdomen, spraying the slower spiders with painful barbed hairs. The entire seething army retreated from the slab. All eyes were on me now. I clambered up onto my victim's stomach—*click-click-click*—teasing his flesh. I have to say; I enjoy commanding an audience.

And, just like the Taliban, I relish the shock factor.

This was no mere torture. This was a special occasion. Until this moment, humans were sure my venom was harmless. But no more. The Taliban had provided me with the gift of destruction, and I was the perfect silent executioner, requiring neither guns nor rockets. In their barren homeland, the saw-scaled viper kills more humans than all other snake species combined. The mujahideen extracted its venom and introduced it into mine. Chemistry, pure and simple. Safe for me to carry, easy for me to deploy.

Soon all other Arachnida would be bred to possess my new secret weapon. This night, here, in this hovel, was the final test. And I was eager to inject it into the old man.

His eyes never left me.

My two-inch-long fangs quivered, savouring the prospect.

And then I sank them deep into his flesh.

As he died, his chest cavity collapsed, folding in on itself as the venom surged through his heart and lungs and bloodstream.

After I had eaten my fill, I stepped back and invited my companions to enjoy their share. Our masters would be well pleased.

Jonathan Boote is Dead

by Mike Rader

IHAD NO choice—his approach had been silent. Besides, my fangs were still deep in the girl's throat. Once Boote recognised me, knew my secret, I had to kill him. Here, under the bridge by the canal, with a broken brick. Surprisingly, there was little blood.

Which made my next task easier.

My father had taught me the importance of the victim's eyes. "They be like them new-fangled cameras. The last thing they see is the killer. So out they must come."

"But, Father—"

"Use your fingers, boy. Nothing to be squeamish about."

Plop. Plop. They were gone.

Just Like Dying Embers

by K.J. Shepherd

THIS IS THE fourth incident involving the burning of churches since the start of last summer. Stay tuned to Ken—" The TV clicked off.

"You don't need to be watching that drivel, my dear. Come, sit with your mom." And I did so. "I bet you're wondering what it all means—the burnings, the chaos, the mayhem…" And I was, so I listened.

"You see, son, these people are lost. They're yearning to love Jesus, like we do, like all good folk do, but they can't find him, for one reason or another. And so they lash out. They hate Jesus because they are lost and can't understand him. They choose violence and hate, and the destruction of holy ground. And for that they will suffer the appropriate punishment."

I waited to hear what that punishment would be. But Momma moved on. She repeated herself a lot, and I wondered if it was part of her disease or just something that she did. She'd been sick for as long as I could remember. Except now she was bald, too. I remember she used to have hair, but that was a while ago now. I wanted to change the topic though, so I asked, "Momma, why can't the doctors fix you?"

She was taken aback. "Well, son, they've certainly tried. With the help of our Lord, they've done remarkable things. And I am ready to accept my fate as the good Lord intends."

"How do you know it's the right fate?"

"You just know, when you're older."

She didn't seem to want to talk about it anymore. I was good at picking up on her mood swings. Then she spoke again.

"You know what the news doesn't tell you?"

I looked up into my mom's deep forest eyes. I shook my head, trying to conceal a tear that had escaped and was running down my cheek.

She cupped my face, and in the same motion, wiped away that tear. "They don't tell you sometimes folk see something in that fire as the embers begin to fade, and the smoke is almost clear."

"What? What do they see?" I asked her.

"Well, now, it's just sometimes, mind you, but I've heard rumours that folk have seen angels in the ruins. Smouldering and glorious and observing all around. Like they're watching, always were watching, but now making themselves known."

She let these words sink into my head.

"Mark my words, there will be divine retribution for those who cross the Lord. But," she said abruptly, making me jump, "it's no good to stay cooped up in here, pondering on these heavy matters. Why don't you take your sister and go play?"

I was about to protest—it'd been rainy lately and would certainly be muddy—but the look in her eyes told me it wasn't really a question. I nodded and sauntered off to find Serene.

***

After I'd convinced Serene to part with her dolls for the evening, we set out from the house. Westward, towards the open fields and hills, away from the houses. And I was right; it was muddy. Even so, we played out by the old smokestacks left abandoned back when Mom was our age, their shadows, like fat fingers, gripping the rolling hillside. They were in such a state of disrepair one was leaning to the point it almost touched another. It was a miracle that it hadn't fallen completely.

My mind dwelled on the fires as Serene did cartwheels down the hill, landing on her backside and laughing all the while. But I didn't join in; my heart wasn't in it.

"Hey," I said after her most recent laughing fit had stopped. "Wanna take a walk with me?"

She nodded breathlessly, hair plastered to her tiny face with sweat.

"I have an idea."

***

When we got to the old church, Serene piped up, "Why are we here, Liam?"

The church's main spire had a plethora of holes in it, and you could see plants actively trying to take it over; bright leaves protruded from its gaping doorways like the earth was reclaiming it.

"I just wanted to see something. You know those fires everyone in town is talking about?" I waited for her to nod. "Well, Mom says there are angels that you can see when one happens, and I need to talk to one."

"What would you ask it?"

I loved that about kids her age—they just took everything at face value.

"I want them to save mom."

Her eyes widened as I pulled the matchbook from my pocket.

"Go find some dry leaves, will you?"

It was all of five minutes before she came back, leaves crumbled up in her small hands. Barely enough shreds remained after she opened her fingers and they came tumbling and blowing out. I sighed. "Just wait here, ok?"

I found some better leaves and some twigs that'd been mercifully untouched by the rain, sheltered beneath a thick canopy of trees. This ought to be enough to draw divine attention. It couldn't take that much.

We went inside the foyer and set up a little pile of dried debris. It took a few matches to get it going. I did like they showed on TV and sheltered the tiny flames with my hands, blowing into it to see the red glow worm across the leaves.

Serene had grabbed a few bibles to burn, but I said that wouldn't be good at all. We didn't want that kind of attention; it's blasphemy, burning the holy word.

While we waited for the fire to catch in the little corner, I went inside to pray properly. It should all work. Everything was coming together. I'd ask God, and the angels when they got here, to fix my mom, and that would be that.

She'd be so proud I'd thought of this all on my own.

The crucifix towered over me as I looked up and swollen light intruded into the dimly lit sanctuary.

Dear God, please come quick and heal my mom. She really likes you, and I love her and want her around for a long time to see me—see us—grow up.

I looked behind me. The front doors were shut. Weird. I looked around and couldn't see anyone else had come in.

"Hello?" My voice echoed back at me six times, as if from unseen ghouls lurking behind the pews. Then silence.

Serene whimpered beside me. I laid my hand on her shoulder, willing her to be quiet.

And I saw a red glow coming from under the door to the foyer, and my breath caught.

I raced to the nearby windows, but they were far too high to reach. Serene looked up at me with vivid eyes. "Stay there," I said as I checked the other side. All the same.

YEAR THREE

That's when the crackle of flames could be heard outside the sanctuary doors.

Hollow were my footsteps as I dashed to the main doors. Frantic were my vain struggles against its stout wooden frame. All for naught; they wouldn't budge. Heart thundering in my chest, I called out to God. And I knew, just as I had known all along, he wasn't there. No one was going to save my momma. And now, no one was going to save us.

I dived and covered my sister. Her wails were haunting. Pleading. Despairing.

"I'm sorry, Liam," she muttered. "I shut it."

"It's ok. Someone will come," I lied.

When the first tendrils of oily smoke came under the door, I started to weep. I patted Serene's head. When the flames roared up the walls, the tears on my face evaporated with the heat. My sister shrieked beneath me. When the cold embrace of death finally pulled me from this raging earth, I was nothing but an ashen husk.

***

And it was rumoured, long after my sister and I burned, that the biggest angel anyone had ever seen was watching over that blaze. The rumour spread—much like a fire does—with a life of its own. It took one neighbourhood first, then the next one. Soon the whole town was talking about it. It was embellished, expanded upon, revised. And it lasted for years after our deaths.

And it gave our mother no comfort at all.

When the Sails Return

by Jennifer Kennett

MOIRA WAS SITTING at her window, its frame crumbling, and glass fractured, looking out across the mist-soaked hills, the sickly green grass sloping here and there. Just beyond the hills she could see the docks. The deep brown of the wooden pier, half rotted, jutting into the ever still sea and the thatched roofs of the Inn's and shops surrounding it doing nothing to break the dismal view. She had spent almost every morning of her life, all nineteen years of it, sitting at that window. Waiting.

"When the sails return so do the sailors, they can take you away so you never come back again," she mumbled the familiar melody. Looking out, she focused on the mist hanging over the horizon. It was so thick, and the clouds so low, she could not tell where the sea ended and the sky began. It was just a lifeless mass of blue and grey.

"When the sails return so do the sailors, they can take you away so you never come back again," she sang. Every girl in Old Town knew the rhyme by heart. When the sails returned, which was only twice a year, all the girls from the town would run, faster than they ever ran, because no one ever knew exactly when the ship would come, towards the

239

docks where they would spend the following week with the sailors who came ashore.

"They are strong and brave; they have sailed the sea. They have battled with monsters of which you have never seen."

Her Grandma said, when she had been a young girl, the docks had been a magical place. There were always ships coming and going bringing exotic objects and people to Old Town. Unfortunately, Moira had never known it be that way; all she knew was the stillness and emptiness. No ships came anymore, except that one ship, creaking but enormous, with masts that reached the clouds and sails the colour of stone. It would dock for a week while the sailors rested and brought supplies for their journey. Then it would leave.

"If they think you are sweet and think your pretty you can go with them to the sea. You will never need return to this Old Town; your life can begin when the sails return. Your life can begin when the sails return."

She saw something black appear on the horizon. She sat upright but soon sat back as she realised it was a flock of birds flying towards land. Moira's grandmother had never understood why anyone would want to leave Old Town despite the fact it only had fields, farms and a dock with no ships.

"If they think you are sweet and think your pretty you can go with them to the sea. You will never need return to this old town; your life can begin when the sails return."

YEAR THREE

A crisp white grey broke the dull horizon and Moira sprung up from her window seat. It slowly grew, it was getting closer. Then she could see the brown of the hull reflected in the sea. The sails had returned.

Moira ran downstairs, past her grandma, who was sleeping in a tattered armchair, and burst out of the hole in the wall where the front door should have been. She ran down the dust road, her tattered tunic billowing behind her. As she came to the fork in the road she could hear three more voices, the other girls had seen it too and were getting nearer. This time, Moira told herself, this time I shall make it aboard. The dust road grew steeper and wider as it wound its way towards the docks and the other girls started pushing each other, wanting to be the first to get to the ship; wanting to be the first to get the sailors attention. That did not matter to Moira though, in fact, she did not want the sailor's attention at all. It was never her intention to wait for one of the sailors to think she was sweet or pretty to take her aboard. No, she was going to sneak on board herself and hide in the hold until the ship reached whatever destination it was bound for.

One year, when she was only fifteen, she had asked one of the sailors—outright asked him—if she could go aboard with them. He had said nothing and merely looked her up and down.

The year after, she had just stormed onto the ship, but as soon as her foot had touched the deck she was being carried off by a sailor, who very forcefully dropped her back onto the pier. That year, the sailors had taken three girls with them, Rebecca, Lileath, and Emily. Emily had been one of Moira's friends, her only friend, and Moira had been surprised when Emily had gone with the sailors, as she had never said she wanted to leave Old Town. She had seemed very happy there. Foolishly, Moira hoped to find Emily again one day and see what exciting and beautiful places she had travelled to, and what new life she had started now she was free from Old Town. Moira had tried to sneak on board every time the ship had landed but had never quite managed to make it aboard. This time it would be different.

As Moira reached the dock, there was a small stream of girls running around the inns and the shops, their speed nearly causing them to fall over as they rounded the corners, all of them headed for the dock.

Moira ran around the side of the inn and stopped, crashing into the back of a group of girls—a crowd of dull tunics staring out to sea. More girls ran up behind Moira and were crashing into the group. The girls in front had stopped because the ship was nearly there. Its sails were so large, moving sharply in the wind. Its hull was robust, and a deep creaking sound filled the air around the dock. Moira could just make out movement on the deck; the sailors.

"Quick, get to your places," Cassandra, a tall thin girl who lived over the next hill to Moira, squealed. The girls scattered, sitting and posing themselves around the dock, trying to make themselves look as sweet and pretty as they could. Moira found a space in amongst some shipping crates, right next to where the ship would moor. She climbed into the pile of boxes; the wood was damp but still scratched her skin. As she settled, trying to keep out of sight, she saw Cassandra rolling her eyes, but Moira didn't care. She had found her spot, somewhere she could hide until night came and the ship would be empty.

A low moaning creak startled Moira as the ship pulled up to the pier. All Moira could see was the deep dark wood of the hull and hear the water crashing as it pulled up into its place. She moved to look out through a gap in the crates. A ramp slammed down onto the pier and Moira could see the sailors departing the ship. Some were tall and some were short, some had thick dark hair, some had no hair at all. The only thing that was the same were the uniforms they wore. Shirts the same stony white as the ship's sails, dark blue tattered trousers and not one sailor wore shoes. They all walked with a careful forcefulness that left Moira tense. She was never quite sure whether or not the sailors would pounce.

***

Moira awoke to the sound of cheerful singing. She had fallen asleep in her hiding place. Rubbing her eyes, she peered through the gap in the crates. Night had fallen hours before and the only light still on was that of the Inn. The sailors were in there.

Slowly she crawled from her hiding place, her muscles aching in protest, her feet and hand so cold that they shook. Stretching out her aching body, she went around the back of the ship, away from the singing and the light. She reached out from the dock, across the water and touched the ship. It felt like it was humming. There was a thick, moss-covered rope hanging down from the deck. She grabbed hold of the rope and pulled herself up but the rope was so hard it cut into her hands where she gripped. Pushing her feet against the damp hull she climbed up to the deck. With what little strength she had left in her aching arms she pulled herself over and landed on her back with a thud. Looking towards the sky where there were no stars as the clouds were so thick, she could see the sails gently swaying in the breeze. Getting to her feet, she could not help but smile. She was on the deck, a there was not a sailor in sight. This was the furthest she had ever gotten onto the ship. Looking around, there was not much on the deck, which surprised her. There was a large, splintered steering wheel, rigging that covered the sails like a spider's web, but not much else. There were no cannons or crow's nest or signs that anyone had ever been aboard.

The wood of the deck was damp and cold, she could feel it through her thin shoes so quickly she descended into the hold. There was only candlelight there, the walls tall and narrow, nothing visible except the ceiling where the candles burned. Moira came to a large door, with a brass handle that was hanging limply by only one nail. She listened but could hear nothing beyond the door. The only sounds were the sea and the creaking of the ship. Carefully she opened the door and through the dim candlelight she saw barrels and crates piled on top of other barrels and crates. She had found the hold.

This would be the perfect place to hide, she thought. It was like a maze. Pulling a candle from the wall she set off into the hold to find somewhere to hide. She turned this way and that until she thought she was far enough away from the door that no one would find her. As she turned around a large barrel marked 'beer' she screamed. There was someone standing there, huddled in the corner facing away. They were short and wore a tattered tunic. They had long pale hair that was damp and clung to the frail body. It was not a sailor; it was a girl.

"Are you alright?" Moira asked, her hand trembling, causing the candlelight to dance around.

The girl turned; cheeks so pale and eyes so dark. When Moira looked at the girl's face, she gasped. It was Emily, exactly as she had looked the last time Moira had seen her when she was fourteen.

"Emily?" Moira said. Was she dreaming, maybe she had fallen asleep in her hiding place again? She blinked hard, trying to wake herself up. Emily stood staring straight at Moira, she was as young as she had been the last time Moira had seen her, but she looked so sickly and weak. Had the sailors kept her locked in the hold all this time?

"They take you away so you never come back," Emily muttered, her cracked lips hardly moving.

"What did you say?" Moira took one step towards Emily. "What happened to you? What have the sailors done to you?"

Emily reached out a pale hand; her fingernails were long and yellowing. Moira reached out too, her hand shaking. As she took hold of Emily's hand all her breath left her body, and she dropped the candle.

"They take you away so you never come back," was all Moira could say, as a chill took her, the candle went out, and she felt the humming of the ship envelop her.

Mirror Image

by Keith R. Burdon

IF THERE WAS anything better in life than going to the cinema, Kevin Mansfield had yet to discover it. Only last week, he had voiced this opinion to his older brother. Dan had smirked and said there were some things better than the cinema.

At the time Kevin was quite put out, then he remembered Dan liked girls, which meant his opinion didn't count, as he obviously didn't have a clue about life.

The cinema was also Kevin's place of escape.

From the moment he walked through the door, he would instantly feel better, shrugging off all his worries about his family, school, everything. He loved every aspect of the visit.

First, there was buying the ticket; watching the ticket seller press a button, then the small, oblong piece of card appearing from the metal plate in the counter. On his first visit, Kevin was firmly convinced there was some kind of tiny person hiding under the counter, feeding the tickets through. At the time, he was both excited and terrified by the thought.

Next up was choosing a snack from the concession stand. Only it wasn't a choice, not really. There was only ever one snack for Kevin—popcorn, and lots of it. If he was honest, he wasn't even that bothered about what film he saw. As long as he was in his seat with a bucket-sized tub of popcorn and something on the screen, he was happy.

The auditorium itself was vast with four separate staircases—two for the stalls, and two for the balcony upstairs. Kevin never bothered with the balcony. That was where the older boys went, usually with girls. Dan told him how they would sit in the back row and hardly ever saw any of the film. Kevin didn't get that at all.

Once inside, he would make straight for the front row, sit with his popcorn bucket in his lap and will the red velvet curtains to open, heralding the start of the film.

He expected today's routine to be no different.

So, it threw him slightly when he saw the ticket seller wasn't Chloe, who was a friend of Dan's and always smiled at Kevin when he bought his ticket. The last time he was here, her smile had caused a funny sensation in his stomach he forgot all about as soon as the film started. Remembering it now, he made a mental note to ask his brother about it later—Dan would know what it was.

Pushing those thoughts to one side, he handed over his money, now giggling at the thought of the little person pushing his ticket up through the slot. Then Kevin saw the replacement ticket seller frowning, and the laughter died in his throat. The old man looked proper scary.

Kevin snatched the ticket and legged it, completely

forgetting his change. This meant he never saw the old man's face start to transform.

Still spooked by the encounter, he nearly forgot to buy popcorn, only remembering as he pushed open the door to the auditorium. Weighing up which was worse—having no popcorn or missing the trailers—he went back to the concession stand.

What the— Yet again, the member of staff was someone different—an old woman. Kevin's mum had always told him using this word was unkind, but the woman was *ugly*. Her face was deeply lined and covered with flakes of dead skin. Kevin stared with grim fascination as she reached up and scratched her chin. Some of the flakes floated down, landing in the popcorn. *Ew, gross*! His stomach lurched. There was no way he was buying that now. *Dead skin flavour popcorn*? *No chance*!

Empty-handed, and now feeling a little jumpy, Kevin pushed through the door and started making his way to his usual spot in the front row. Something else was wrong. It only took a moment for him to realise he was the only person in there.

Usually, something like this would be extra special. Having the entire space to himself...that was *beyond* exciting! Today, however, it made him feel scared.

And then all the lights dropped completely.

Kevin clamped a hand over his mouth to keep in the scream that was threatening to escape. He dashed for the door, stumbling in the darkness.

The part of his brain that loved films wasn't at all surprised to find it was locked. The part that was an eleven-year-old child was absolutely terrified. He rattled the door, desperately hoping it would open if he just pulled hard enough.

He looked over his shoulder, expecting to see some kind of monster, a shadow in the darkness. Instead, he saw the screen flicker into life.

There was his house.

Kevin closed his eyes. This wasn't happening. Almost against his will, he opened them again. On the screen was a close-up of his smiling face. The camera cut away to a blurred shot. Focusing, it slowly revealed the front doors of a cinema. This cinema.

As terrified as he was, Kevin also felt something else. He was *excited*. Here he was, a star in his own film. How cool was that? Transfixed, he reached out and his hand felt the back of one of the seats. He sat down, never taking his eyes off the screen.

The footage had reached the point where he had bought the ticket. The camera remained on the face of the old man after the boy had run away. Kevin's eyes grew wide as he saw the face on the screen start to change. The special effects were amazing. A voice in his head asked, "What if it's real?" He ignored it.

The camera followed on-screen Kevin as he

approached the auditorium, then it panned around to show him heading back to the concession stand. Another close-up showed the look of disgust on his face as he watched the old woman. The camera withdrew to show Kevin turning away, then it swung back to focus on the old woman as she continued to scratch. Livid streaks began to appear under her fingernails. Droplets of blood formed, rolling over her ruined face to splash on to the popcorn below.

The voice in Kevin's head was now screaming, shouting at him to get out. Try the door again, anything, just get out! His body refused to react to the impulses his brain was sending. He couldn't move.

The film continued. Kevin watched the events leading to this very moment. On the screen, as they had done in reality just moments before, the lights went out. The camera switched to night vision, giving everything an unearthly green glow. He watched as on-screen Kevin stumbled, then saw the panic on his face as he tried and failed to open the door.

He willed himself to move, but still his body refused. Was it his imagination or could he feel something holding his legs in place? He began to whimper, tears leaking from the corners of his eyes.

On the screen, he saw the back of his head and what looked very much like the glint of a blade.

The stereo sound of his scream was shockingly loud in the empty auditorium.

BLACK HARE PRESS

Snow Wraiths

by Maggie D. Brace

AS I BENT to release Archie, the lead dog, from his harness, I caught a quick glimpse of movement beneath the snow's crust. Shrugging it off as merely the blinding squall whirling about us, I finished unharnessing the rest of the pack. In the blizzard, I could barely make out Archie, ever in command, leading his team to their shed. Struggling against the onslaught of wind and snow, I slowly followed. I spent a while inspecting the dogs' paws for injuries or signs of frostbite before continuing our nightly ritual by feeding and bedding them down, making sure each dog got a few moments of petting and attention. Of course, Archie had been my favourite for years, so I had an extra moment or two cuddling with him.

Leaving the shed door slightly ajar, I began the hundred yards to my cabin. Not wanting to get blown off course, I reached out for the guide wire that connected the two buildings and slowly slogged my way forwards. About halfway there, I felt a sharp pain in my left calf. I winced and stumbled, but thinking it was only a muscle spasm, I carried on.

Two steps later, my right hamstring exploded in pain.

Crumpling in a heap, I let go of the guide wire to clutch at my thigh. Through the flurrying snow, I could make out a pool of blood forming beneath me. Willing myself to stand, I clawed about in search of the wire, but couldn't manage to grasp it. I decided to move forward, gauging the way home, realising the below zero temperature would surely kill me before I bled out.

Limping, I managed a few dozen steps before a high-pitched whine pierced the air next to my ear. Feebly swatting in the sound's direction, I cursed as something took a chunk of flesh out of my cheek. Numb with fear, I forced myself to move forward. I began limping faster, flailing my arms around. Another whining sound preceded a large hunk of flesh being ripped off my nose. I could taste the salty blood coursing down my face, and I spat it out in dismay.

Teetering another few steps, my heart sank as I made out the frozen pool of blood from where I had first fallen down—I had been walking in circles and was no closer to my cabin. I was close to giving up all hope when a dark shape hurtled into view.

It was Archie, snapping and pawing at our unseen foe. He seemed able to sense the hidden creature. Horrified, I saw his hind leg snap in two in the scuffle, the bone piercing through his flesh. Archie yelped in pain but continued to do battle.

A whining retreated into the blizzard, and Archie collapsed to the ground, whimpering and licking at the exposed bone. That was the final straw. I scooped the dog up, churned my way back toward the shed, and pulled the door shut. In the dim light I could see Archie's upturned face, almost smiling at me. He licked my hand.

Together, we had fought the snow wraith, and won.

Vengeance

by Mel Andela

TRICK OR TREAT." The childlike voice floats down the darkened street. The sidewalks are empty, costumed youngsters long since gone home. It was far too late even for trouble-seeking teens, yet the voice was there, repeating.

"Trick or treat." The singsong words pierce his ears, a cold sweat beading on his temples. The voice is familiar; he recalls that Halloween, and the news reports about her disappearance for months after. No one had ever suspected him.

He watches a shadow approach his door, a small claw-like hand raking down the window.

"Trick or treat," it demands in a hollow rasp.

Hal Owen

by Steven Holding

INTRODUCING MR OWEN (Hal to his friends, if he had any…). Date of birth: October thirty-first.

Born ugly as sin, but it's how he was treated that paved the way for later behaviour, not what's within. Beaten and abused, he decided to choose a suitably horrifying revenge against those who had wronged him.

Every birthday, he slips out into the night, frightful features finally fitting in as he stalks, slices and dices one unlucky trick or treater, only to disappear for another year.

One night.

One life.

A tradition begun aged seventeen.

This year Hal turns seventy-three.

He's still sprightly.

Last Kiss

by Caoimhin Kennedy

MY DAUGHTER KISSES me. "Heading home," she says.

Since my cancer, Carrie gives out my treats on Halloween.

I roll my wheelchair to the porch's edge and watch her taillights dwindle into the night. That's when I see the girl on my lawn.

"Hello," the little girl says. She's dressed as a goat.

"No more candy, I'm afraid!"

"Quite alright," she answers. "Tell me, did you enjoy your last kiss with your daughter?"

Her eyes go ablaze.

I gape. "You've come for me…"

The Devil smirks childishly, in the distance a horn blares; metal crunches, "No. Not for you."

YEAR THREE

Pumpkin Head

by Pauline Yates

I'VE WON 'BEST Halloween Display' two years running, but while hanging decorations, my new neighbour distracts me. He likes my legs. I love his wide smile. Tempted, I suggest a private trick or treat before the judges arrive.

Invitation accepted, he asks what tricks I know. I show him my wax pumpkin heads. "They're moulded with a machete," I say as his head drops to the floor. The trick is finding the right shape. His head is perfect. Dunking him in wax, I carve out his wide smile and hang him next to the previous neighbours; a winning hat trick.

Harvest

by Elle Jauffret

SHE ALWAYS PICKED the ugliest pumpkin, the rotten one with the mouldy skin—disfigured, putrid, and asymmetrical.

She would carve through its decomposing shell with sharp nails—and dig through its flesh with bare hands.

Once its entrails removed, she would search through the stringy pulp for the blackest of seeds that she could plant.

She would sow them in the freshly ploughed ground of the paupers' grave where Jane and John Does were buried, forgotten.

She would spit on the soil and chant in tongues. So that a year later, on October 31st, monsters would rise from its sprouts.

Halloween at the Morrison's

by Sophie Wagner

IN MATEO'S OPINION, Halloween was the best time of the year. On decorating day, his family would carve, hang skeletons and Mother would make meat pies.

Sadly, this year they started without him.

When he arrived home, Morrie was already carving a lopsided smile into a decapitated head. In the kitchen, Mother was busy chopping the rest of the body. He could already smell the pies in the oven.

"Sorry to start without you," his dad called. "But you can join your brother, if you want."

Mateo advanced on the bound man in the corner.

"Don't mind if I do."

Fresh Start

by Andrew Anderson

THE DOORBELL RANG.

"So it begins," muttered Ed, getting up to answer the door for his inaugural trick-or-treaters.

This was Ed's first Halloween since moving to town, so he'd prepared a tray of rather lopsided homemade cakes, along with some assorted chocolates and lollies from the supermarket.

These kids were polite; not wishing to offend him, they grabbed a cake each and as much wrapped sugar as their buckets could carry. Ed knew they would wait until they were out of sight, then toss his cakes into the hedge.

That's why he'd put the poison into the store-bought candy instead.

Kid Tax

by Michelle Brett

HAND OVER THE candy, kid."

Anthony trembled beneath the bully's gaze. He clutched his basket closer and spluttered out some words.

"Please, no. It took me ages."

The bully snorted, then glanced back at his cronies; their faces already stuffed with stolen treats.

"Now," he hissed.

Anthony dropped the basket as he held back his tears. He ran from the alleyway, laughter following him out.

But once he'd turned the corner, the run became an amble. His superhero cape floated behind him in the wind.

Not long now.

Soon they'd start gorging themselves, then the poison would take its toll.

Trick or Eat

by Emily Carlson

BEING LEFT HOME alone on Halloween was the worst. Too old to trick or treat, too young to accompany her parents to whatever monster mash they were attending this year.

When the doorbell rang, she sighed, dragging the bowl of candy over to answer.

Three masked people rushed at her, holding knives out and pushing their way into her house. They crowded around, threatening her if she didn't comply.

She smiled at the intruders, relishing the turn of their confidence to panic when sharp fangs emerged from her gums.

Maybe being stuck at home this year wouldn't be so bad.

All Hungry Ghosts' Eve

by Collin Yeoh

HALLOWEEN? *REALLY*, GRANDDAUGHTER? You can't speak your mother tongue. You scorn our ways and traditions. You threw yourself at the first white man who could say "*ni hao*." You don't even have an altar to me in your home.

Now you eagerly celebrate this stupid Western drivel with its vulgar costumes and its children's games?

You forget we have our own Hungry Ghost Festival. On that night the gates of hell open—and unlike this meaningless, commercialised holiday—that is when spirits really do walk the earth.

I'll be paying you a visit then.

And I'll be *very* hungry.

Trick or Treat

by N.E. Rule

SARAH OPENS THE door with her baby tucked at her hip. A teenager brandishing a top hat greets her.

"You're a bit old," she chides. "What're you supposed to be?"

"I'm a magician." His charming smile is infectious.

She smiles back. "What's your trick then?"

"How about a disappearing act?" He waves his hands 'abracadabra' style.

"Sure." She waits.

"Not now. Maybe next week?"

Sarah looks back confused, so he continues, "Definitely within the month." His finger trails down the baby's nose. "But won't you miss him?"

Speechless, she pushes the candy bowl into his arms and slams the door.

Peter, Peter, Pumpkin Eater

by L.J. McLeod

THE PUMPKIN OPENED its eyes. It had never had eyes before. Images flooded its awareness, visions of its Maker wielding the knife that had carved out its new existence. A nose followed and waves of aroma filled the pumpkin. When the Maker added a mouth, it began to feel joy. Then a hand pushed into its mouth and the pumpkin's joy turned to horror. Heat flared deep inside, and the smell of its own cooking flesh was overwhelming. In panic, it bit down. A gush of blood quenched the burning. The Maker screamed and the pumpkin found itself wanting more.

Three Simple Rules

by Leanbh Pearson

ONLY THREE SIMPLE rules: Never walk alone in the forest. Never follow robed figures carrying red candles. Never open the door to the *ánimas*. Darkness was their domain—the condemned who wander Spain in purgatory.

A knock at the door, and she thought again how insidiously commercialised Halloween was.

Heart pounding, opening the door, she sighed with relief. Not the *ánimas*.

A young boy in a Frankenstein costume held out a bag, waiting. Dropping two chocolates into it, she noticed the black-robed parents. The red candles, cowls not hiding rotted flesh. Condemned to join them, she'd broken rule three.

Sweet Delicious Candy

by John Ward

S HE COULD SMELL candy on the evening breeze.

She closed her eyes and let the intoxicating perfume wash over her, rekindling memories of bygone nights filled with jack-o'-lanterns and costumes and excitement.

The mouth-watering scent lured her to a bustling suburban street where the candy ran freely. Drunk with anticipation, she sank her teeth into a discarded treat and gorged herself, savouring the sweet ichor as it exploded on her tongue.

She retreated before the enraged man was upon her. Looking back as she fled, she saw him try vainly to stop the blood gushing from the child's severed artery.

Make It Last

by Birgit K. Gaiser

GROWN-UPS ALWAYS ASK where my parents are. I mumble, "They couldn't come." They know that's code for a challenging home environment, so they put some extra treats in my pumpkin bag.

I look past them through the door, imagining what it's like to live there.

Finally, when the pumpkins have gone dark, I return to my favourite house.

I knock. A woman opens.

In a small voice, I ask: "May I come in?"

Full of concern, she nods. Lifts me up. Hugs me.

I nibble her neck and drink—just a little. If I'm careful, she'll last until next year.

Ghost Dog

by Maggie D. Brace

OUR FIRST SPACEWALK loomed in front of us as we slowly got our space legs under us. We were not deterred by the stories of creepy occurrences spun by the veterans, we were simply anxious to get this experience under our belt.

Sergie and I had done simulation walks as a team multiple times, and were pretty excited, but also understandably nervous.

Finally, it was time to go, and all went well till a chill ran down my spine as if someone or something were watching us. Turning to Sergie, I saw a look of sheer terror on his face. My eyes followed his pointing finger and saw what looked to be a small astronaut from the early Space Age hovering near me.

As the form slowly spun around, I got a chilling glimpse of the remains of Laika, our trusty space dog, seconds before it grazed my shoulder. Coldness coursed through me, as Laika's dog ghost entered my soul.

Breathe

by Delfina Bonuchi

MY LUNGS BURNED and my head pounded, but she just watched from afar as I writhed.

Breathe.

Her dark eyes—ebony pools—pleaded, but her smile was wide, sharp teeth glinting in the diffused light.

Breathe.

I reached out, movements slow and tortured, but she dodged and dived, fins flashing.

Breathe, she whispered without words from close behind, just as darkness began to curl at the edges of my world.

Breathe, she bellowed, face close to mine, and I sucked in a great lungful of salty water.

Then, as I closed my eyes one last time, she finally kissed me.

The Submission Process

by Avery Hunter

THEY QUEUE.

With gaunt faces and bloodshot eyes, weary feet trudge slowly. The line snakes down the hill, back and forth between the Hellfires, all eyes on the stooped shoulders in front. Silence, but for quiet groans.

He watches.

Three crimson eyes glow eerily in the dark; all that can be seen of the black Hellhare as he waits in the shadows.

Trembling hands lift their offering to the altar, reverently placing it upon the last. Some even shed a single tear.

His soul aches.

For he—the editor—knows he is the maker of dreams, and the breaker of hearts.

Keep Out

by John Lane

CHILLS RAN THROUGH billy's body underneath the white cotton bedspread. Thoughts of staying at the Lizzie Borden house in her old room frightened him, but his thrill-seeking father, Charles, insisted.

He slept after tossing and turning all night.

At 9:30am, Billy awoke to what sounded like a watermelon being hacked open.

In what was once Andrew Borden's room lay the unrecognisable face of Charles. Blood poured through the impressions made by a blade, or an axe.

Then, sirens wailed.

Arrested on circumstantial evidence, Bill was escorted into a police car. He noticed the ghostly transparent image of Lizzy waving back.

Voice in the Wind

by S. Jade Path

SARAH WOKE HUNGRY. Shuffling over to the hearth, she stirred the embers and added a new log. As she turned to reach for the kettle, the sky outside the window pulled her attention, and she immediately forgot the pot in her hand.

All week, the sun had been shining—trying to anyway—its watery light drizzling through winter's grey haze. The snow had been nothing but flurries, the light breeze setting them to skittering around the fence line in gentle gusts. She'd heard the winds picking up last night; felt the slightest draft as she walked past the cabin's front door.

A single glance out her window at the morning sky, and Sarah knew they were in trouble. The horizon was gone. Just gone. Lost in a line of darkness that had nothing to do with the early hour. Breakfast will have to wait.

"Jean! Jean! Wake up!"

Jean—ever dutiful—woke. Staring, mostly without hearing, as his wife spoke with uncharacteristically animated expressions and gesticulating hands. He was vaguely wondering what she was on about this early—and why there was no scent of coffee—when a single word

275

made it through his sleep-hazed thoughts. Storm. It caught his wandering attention and his body jolted upright. It's too early for storms. The earliest should be weeks out yet. We aren't ready! Sweeping aside the sleeping furs he had been so snuggly wrapped in, Jean flung himself into his breeches, knotting the ties of his fur-lined boots as he all but fell out of the bed in his haste.

Standing still, Sarah watched in astonishment as her husband leaped about. Choosing not to comment, she instead walked over to the rack near the door, gathering up the hunting supplies for her husband. When he had calmed enough to take a breath, she helped him into his buckskin and fur wrappings.

"Now, don't worry. I'll see to the chickens and the cow, and the cellar supplies." A kiss on the cheek, and she sent him off to find whatever game, or fish, could be found quickly. Shutting the door behind her, she stepped out into the wintry stillness. The sharp winds of the night before had ceased, the snow had stopped falling, and the birds in the branches were eerily silent. A shiver danced down her spine, the fine hairs at her nape standing up.

But Sarah had little patience for omens, superstitions, and tall tales. Living out here, between the Two Rivers and the wild, there was no time for such nonsense. Adjusting her skirts in irritation, she strode off to check on the chickens.

The hens huddled deep into their nests, barely a cluck between them, even as Sarah plucked the few eggs from beneath them. Even the old rooster was quieter than was usual. Melba, sweet heifer that she was, stood docile enough for her milking—each plash into the pail rang in the air like a gunshot. Sarah stood, her nerves jangling, to refresh the cow's feed and water. Next, mucking out the stall and laying in enough hay to keep it warm through the storm.

Gathering the mostly empty egg basket and the full milk pail, Sarah high-tailed it across the yard to the cabin. Pausing to knock the worst of the slush from her boots, she glanced around before darting back into her stout home. Setting the eggs and milk down by the door, she wrapped her arms around herself, trying to convince herself it was only the cold, nothing more. Only the cold, not the approaching dark, bringing with it an icy dread. Not a fear of the dark itself, but of the primal certainty that she did not want to be outside in the brittle stillness when the dark arrived.

Sarah swore under her breath as the slam of the front door nearly caused her to drop one of the preserved food jars from their tiny hoard. She called out to Jean, "I'll be up in a minute." Sarah took a moment to set upright the jar, and store the eggs and milk, and another to right her skirts, and tuck away an errant lock of hair before climbing the cellar stairs.

A brace of rabbits lay on the table, the meagre reward of a day's effort. Sarah sighed but got to work. As absent as the wildlife has been all day, I should be grateful for these.

Ten heavy thwacks separated legs, tails, and heads. In the time it took Jean to stack wood in the fireplace and stoke a new fire, Sarah's swift knife work had reduced the two rabbits into three neat piles: neatly butchered sections of meat and bone, a wet heap of offal leaking blood and fluids onto the table; and two nearly perfect skins, with small bits of blood-stained fur clumping together.

The rising winds made it hard to hear and Jean finally resorted to mime to make clear his intention to bring in a supply of firewood. The lean-to against the cabin was well stocked, and three trips had a goodly supply lain in to dry next to the hearth.

With the animals cared for, and food and firewood accounted for, there was nothing left to do as the storm at last broke, shattering the stillness. The world wrapped in the blinding white. Sarah and Jean sat before the fire, settled in to wait out the storm, sure it would wane in a day, maybe two.

***

But it didn't end the next day. Or the day after that. Or the day after that. Day followed night, followed day, until it was only darkness and skirling winds. Around the eaves the winds raced, mournful as the voices of the damned, unceasing and eerie. Branches whipped against the cabin, skeletal fingers clawing at the windows and the door. The fire was dying, icy tendrils snake through the flue.

All these days the livestock had been quiet. When the

silence was shattered, they felt it as much as heard. The minutes of sudden panicked squawking and crowing from the henhouse were disquieting. The bovine scream was utterly unnerving.

The abrupt silence was even worse.

Jean didn't go to check on them. The fear of the storm had prevented him from tending to them this last week. Now, fear of what was out in the storm kept him indoors. Another night passed in cold and worry. Waiting for the snow to stop. Waiting for the wind to cease. Anxieties building by the hour. The firewood had dwindled to a bare handful of logs. They were out of food—the rabbits long since eaten, and the jars from the cellar emptied. They would have to brave the storm tomorrow. But fear coloured their thoughts and stayed their feet; it took three days for "tomorrow" to come.

***

That morning dawned cold and still—the lack of wind was deafening in its silence. Jean stood before the door, his hands clenched at his sides, trying to stem their shaking. Sarah fidgeted behind him, apron wrinkling in her twisting fingers. Gathering up his courage, he grasped the doorknob, twisting it and quickly stepping out into the empty whiteness.

The henhouse door stood half open; hinges bent at awkward angles. Blood scent hung heavy in the air, despite the numbing cold. Jean pushed the door open fully. The wooden walls painted thickly in streaks of black gore, feathers poking through chunks of red ice; all that remained of the chickens. Jean stumbled back, retching.

Jean looked over at the cowshed and involuntarily shook his head, knowing on some level what he would find. Needing food supplies, and hoping against hope that what he feared he would find was just in his imagination, he crept tentatively into the shed, careful to keep his back to the wall—as if that would somehow make it safer.

With every inhale, the cold stabbed at his lungs with icy needles. Each heartbeat throbbing violently within his chest. The crunch of snow under his boots rang loud in his own ears, causing his head to swivel; on a constant search for whoever—or whatever—had disembowelled his chickens.

Poor Melba was gone. The largest identifiable chunk— a section of ribcage—bore teeth marks, clear on the exposed bone. A mandible lay half buried in the hay. The stall splashed with blood, small spatters of flesh clinging to the rough timbers. Shreds of intestine dangle from the water trough—grotesque, scarlet icicles. As Jean stood transfixed, his brain rejecting the horror before him, one of the intestine pieces slipped. The icicle plunged downward, piercing a forgotten eyeball with an audible squelch. Jean screamed. He screamed without stopping.

Jean's wails finally gave way to muttering as Sarah set him in front of the fire, safely back in their home with a glass of whiskey in hand. The whiskey scorched his raw throat but numbed the images in his head. He quaffed it in a single gulp.

Sarah had seen little of what was in the stall, just a vague impression of red and ice. The stench of raw, rancid meat had hit her hard. Nearly dropping her to her knees. Grasping Jean by the shoulder of his coat, she guided him out of the shed and into the cabin. She cast a nervous glance at her husband—she'd never seen him so pale, so deathly pale. The whiteout conditions picked back up outside. Sarah shivered.

It was late the next day before he spoke, still in his place near the fire. "It wasn't natural. Whatever did that to Melba…it wasn't natural. No bear, no wolf… Nothing eats…savages… Not…not like that." He spoke, but not to Sarah—it was as if the words had wandered out while his mind was off elsewhere. It was two days more before he roused himself.

***

They were out of food—had been for days. Sarah had managed to pull in what firewood remained against the cabin, and forage from around the trees closest to the house. But they needed food—a caribou would be perfect, but more rabbit, even a root vegetable, or a handful of nuts would do at this point. Jean donned his coat and his furs, grabbed his hunting gear, kissed his wife, and stepped into the stinging snow and wind.

BLACK HARE PRESS

Sarah settled in with her sewing. The bubbling up of fear, for Jean out there, for herself alone, drove her to her feet to pace. She fiddled with the fire, sat to work on some embroidery. Jean's voice, screaming her name, sent her bolt upright and racing out the door. Sheer habit found her cloak in her hand, with the open door banging shut behind her.

"Jean!" His voice had come from the edge of the property. The sun was low in the sky as she ran toward the tree line. Trying to follow his voice, still calling her name. "Jean?" She darted out among the trees, his voice hard to distinguish from the wind, the rustling firs, and scraping of the birch branches. The sameness of the forest and the spinning snows were disorienting. Soon she was lost and frightened. The voice had changed, gained a sibilance that was not Jean's. Too late she realised the danger.

A shadow detached from the trees, its stretched form gaunt, starved. Long fingers curving into talons. Eyes so deep set as to seem like vacant pools of malevolence. Her back pressed hard into the bark behind her. Sarah heard its antlers rasping against the branches above her. The sound reminded her of the night the livestock died. It had been the trees scraping against the cabin that night…right? The voice continued to call her, but it wasn't coming from the forest anymore, and it was no longer her name being called. It was inside her head and its call was one of hunger. Sarah stood enthralled as the creature leaned down toward her, its serrated teeth chittering, iron and spoiled meat heavy on its breath. One curved talon stroked her cheek.

Then it was gone.

Sarah stood there, trembling, for minutes that moved like days. Then she ran, unerring, back to the cabin and a concerned Jean. He had returned home empty-handed and apologetic. Sarah didn't care. She knew where all the game had gone. She had met the forest's new master, and he was famished.

Jean went to bed early, having exhausted himself in his futile hunting. Sarah sat by the hearth, rocking back and forth. When his breathing evened out, indicating he was fast asleep, Sarah rose. Compelled by the voice in the wind, she grabbed a knife and moved toward the bed, carefully pulling back the covers. For the first time, Sarah saw her husband, not as man but as meat. An extra-large hare. The remnants of Sarah skittered back into the corner of her mind, pushed back by the driving voice.

An expert slice opened his throat; the hot spray coated her hand and spilled down the front of her dress. Looking at her knife, she knew it wasn't up to the next task. Striding over to the fireplace, she picked up the axe. Five precise chops separated legs and arms from the body. She set the head to one side and blood quickly soaked into the bedding. Picking up the knife again, she made short work of opening the belly, spilling gore down the side of the bed, and separating the ribs from the spine. By sunrise she had rent the meat from bone and sat before the dying fire—she no

longer felt the cold—gnawing on the last rib.

Hunger assuaged, the residuum of Sarah surfaced long enough to sob; the tears carving icy tracks through the bloody smears around her mouth. Glancing over her shoulder at what remained of her husband: a pile of tattered clothing; a wet slop of skin on the table; his head, still lolling against the bed pillow, shocked eyes staring. Pulling her gaze back to the fire did nothing to alleviate her horror. Strewn across the hearthstone were the bones—some with wet gobbets of flesh still clinging. Weeping, the last of Sarah fled into her mind and was subsumed by the Wendigo.

The storm still raged outside, and the voice in the wind still hungered. She still hungered.

Hungry…

Hungry…

Hungry…

The Unleashing

by Maggie D. Brace

THERE WAS THAT confounded sound again!

Slowly honing in on the squeak emanating from the bowels of his house, Elijah peered resolutely into the darkness below his stairs. Perhaps just a trick of the light, but a glint caught his eye. He hunkered lower and squeezed his girth into the tight space. Clamouring with outstretched fingers, he felt a rectangle inscribed in the floor. Prying it up, he pondered, *could this be some kind of oubliette?*

He leaned forwards for a view down the hole, recoiling as chilled air blasted through and past him.

The trapped spirit shrieked in delight.

Family Cave

by Mike Rader

I T'S JUST A cave," I argued, peering along the wind-whipped shore toward the gash in the cliff. "What's there to see?"

"Trust me," Anna said.

We trudged along the path, raw gusts howling around us. The Firth of Forth was a broad expanse of icy grey water to our left. White caps broke its surface. A winter vacation on the west coast of Scotland was all my wife's idea. Yes, its rugged beauty was unique, just as she said it would be. Breathtaking. Timeless. But bitterly cold. We'd hiked two miles that morning, north from Ballantrae, next stop Girvan, but she'd insisted on making this stop.

We reached the mysterious gap in the cliff. The forbidding headland towered above. Bald, craggy. Tufted grass flattened by arctic blasts. I gripped my fluttering map with both hands. "It's called Bennane Head," I told her.

"Yes, Bennane," Anna repeated softly, as though the name had some special significance.

She pointed to the wet, glistening rock above the cave entrance. "See, Alan. That's how high the water gets at high tide."

A burst of wind stirred the coarse sand at my feet. The

cold bit deep. I glanced at the shiny rock. "So the cave is covered by the sea?" I scowled. "Glad we're not in there."

"Not yet," she said, adjusting the strap on her backpack. She clambered over the tumbled rocks toward the cave.

"No way!" I called. "Come back, Anna!"

Sometimes my wife has wild ideas.

"Alan, what's the matter with you?" She turned to speak as if I were a naughty child. "I've read all about this cave. It's covered at high tide, but it's not dangerous. Inside, the tunnels run for a mile beneath the headland, well above the water level."

"Sounds a good place to keep out of," I tossed back.

But Anna was determined. "Ten minutes," she said. "That's all I ask."

So I followed her over the jumble of rocks to the entrance. Inky pools of water dotted the floor of the cave. Anna flicked on a flashlight and moved deeper inside. Graffiti covered the walls. Suddenly I could tell we were climbing, as the broad tunnel rose higher inside the headland.

"You could hide an army in here," I said lightly.

"They did."

I glanced across at Anna. "Who did?"

"Well, not exactly an army. A family. Generations of them."

The steep tunnel seemed endless. The ground was as

dry as a bone. Clearly, we were well above the high tide level.

"Anna, nobody would live in here," I challenged.

Anna laughed. "In the 1600s, Sawney Bean and his wife Black Agnes did. And their forty-five children."

I stopped dead in my tracks. A dim memory stirred. "I think I've heard of them."

"They were cannibals," Anna explained. "They preyed on lonely travellers. Ambushed them on the roads. Brought them back here. Killed and ate one thousand people over twenty-five years."

"Charming," I scoffed.

"It took the King of Scotland and hundreds of troops to hunt them down," Anna insisted. "It's true."

"It's a legend, is all," I reminded her. Glancing at my wristwatch, I said, "Your ten minutes is up, darling."

I turned to leave, but Anna clutched my arm.

"Don't you want to see where they lived?" she demanded.

"Anna, even if the legend were true, there'd be nothing left to see after all these years."

Her grip tightened. She tugged my sleeve. "Alan, just another minute," she whispered.

We rounded a turn into a small side passage. Anna froze. "I feel I've been here before," she said.

I fought to control my patience. "You were born in New York," I reminded her. "And this is your first trip to

Scotland, isn't it?"

"I know that, but I also know our family did come from this region, Ayrshire, a couple hundred years ago."

"Anna, for God's sake!" I burst out laughing. "You're not descended from cannibals."

Anna entered a cavern to one side. Her face paled. She shivered. "They *were* here, Alan. *I swear it!*"

Something inside me snapped. "Hey, come on, Anna, let's go. You're freaking me out!"

She pulled away, darted deeper into the cavern, searching the shadows, pushing aside small rocks. She turned, holding a long dagger.

The hilt was rusted, but the blade gleamed. "Explain this, Alan. Explain how I knew where to find this!"

My temper flared. "I can't. It's a coincidence. Or some hiker left it there for a joke. Anna, let's go!"

She pressed a finger against the blade, drew blood. Her tongue licked it away. "After all those years, it's still so sharp."

"I guess because the air is dry in here," I offered. "Let's go!"

She reached out and took my hand. "Alan, do you believe in the supernatural? Like, some people can take over other people?"

"What are you talking about?" Anna was the most rational woman I'd ever met. I couldn't believe what she was saying. "Honestly, Anna, you don't believe in stuff like that. You never have!"

The sudden pain was swift. Excruciating. I screamed.

The knife was slicing through one of my fingers.

"Anna!" I shouted in agony.

I couldn't pull my hand clear. Her grip was like steel.

Her eyes flamed. "You're wrong, Alan. Someone from the past can reach someone in the present."

The pain was agonising as the knife hacked into sinew. "Anna, stop it! You've gone mad!"

I tried to thrust her aside, but some unseen power held me pinned to the wall. She raised the knife and held it to my throat.

She held my gaze. "Did you know that when they executed Sawney Bean, he said: 'It isn't over...it will never be over...' I believe him, Alan. I understand what he meant. I learned that some of the Bean family survived, went to the colonies in America. They kept eating strangers wherever they travelled. They never lost their taste for human flesh."

"Anna, my love," I begged. "What has happened to you?"

"I am here to continue the family tradition."

Which is when I remembered: Anna's maiden name was—

"Just because your name was Bean, doesn't mean anything!" I tried to reason with her. It was futile. Who was this woman I'd married? This beautiful woman with insanity blazing in her wild eyes?

YEAR THREE

Then I screamed louder, as she got to work hacking through a second finger.

Paying the Piper

by M. Leigh

THE PIPE QUIVERS against blistered lips as he plays the familiar, melancholy tune. The song slinks through the forest, reaching the sleeping village, and tickles the children's ears awake. Naked feet scurry toward the windows.

He approaches.

The Piper's pointed boots click along the cobblestone below bloodied green and white striped pantaloons. His face—mangled shadows, masked by a feathered cap.

The children know what was promised—the wicked deal made by the elders. Their sinful debt.

Watching their parents file behind the Piper, following his hypnotic stride away from town, they smile.

Children know how to make deals, too.

No Lady

by Tracy Davidson

SOME CALL ME myth. Others believe. None get my story right.

I've lived a thousand lives, in many forms.

I've waited and watched as humans developed and spread. I've loved them. I've hated them. Or, rather, hated what they have done to this world. What they still do.

My purpose is to protect. But not them. They have doomed themselves. Left unchecked, they will doom all. Time to stop waiting and watching.

I leave my lake behind. My arms morph into swords, ready to slice through the true monsters of this world.

My name is Excalibur. My legend begins anew.

It's Worse the Second Time 'Round

by C.L. Sidell

WE ABANDONED WILL at camp—packed our belongings whilst he sweated hallucinations. The risk of contracting fever was too great.

Three days later, we were shocked to find him waiting for us at the station.

"Jake," he said with a nod. "Lyle."

From atop the passenger car, a gigantic snow-white bird released a sonorous cry, an ant-like trail of smoke escaping its beak.

The vapour invaded my nostrils, turned my legs to jelly. Lyle hacked up blood.

"You reap what you sow," Will declared, boarding the train.

And the creature, emitting a series of caws, flapped its wings and disappeared.

Kuntilanak

by Pauline Yates

DRUNK ON SAMSU, I muddle the warning about a white-dressed woman with long, lank hair. Who said that? The bartender? No, a Malaysian beggar; a story for a coin, he said as I staggered home.

A generous man, I obliged, and learned about the mythical Kuntilanak, a vengeful female spirit who lures unsuspecting men and feasts on their organs, her wickedness driven by the stillborn soul she cannot birth. "She reeks of frangipani. Smell that boy, you run, run…" I shuddered. 'Twas a good story.

Continuing, I meet a woman, lost, alone. I stop to help; her frangipani-perfume is irresistible…

La Sihuanaba

by Xavier Garcia

IT'S FIVE TO midnight and I'm nowhere when I see her, dressed in white; a blushing bride.

She's not here to give me anything like the life growing inside my wife's tummy, just the birthing of maggots in my gut.

And yet, how sweet would it be to taste her lips, to feel the soft press of her against me.

So, I go to her.

Go, so we may say our black vows to one another; a wedding ceremony attended by no one, officiated by an indifferent moon, and consummated with all the promise of euphoric rot and everlasting silence.

We Ride Through the Night

by Tim Law

WE RIDE THROUGH the night, my master and I. At witch's summons we arise from the pumpkin's patch, sabre drawn and jack-o'-lantern head. We search until our quarry is found and then the race begins.

This part I love the most, the thrill of the chase. We ride across land we know by heart. Soon, like a frightened hare our quarry is cornered. Then thwack, we harvest the head of the witch's foe and lay it at her farmhouse door.

Then back to the earth and worms we return until we hear the witch's chant. She summons us once more.

Crossroads

by Rachel Reeves

SWEAT SOAKS THE man's shirt, breaking his pale skin into tomato blotches. He scrabbles in the crossing, nails cracking in the sun. The box was here; the whispered stories had to be true.

"Searching for salvation, stranger?"

The scrabbling man stops and smooths his shirt, every bit the contrite child.

"Salvation? Naw, I passed salvation a while ago."

"I can see that, stranger. You are stealing from my stoop, after all."

Stealing? He's never—

He's bitten through his tongue, tasting rust and dripping red.

"Speak, sinner."

The Other never loses His smile as the man drops and the dust drinks.

Quota

by D. Kershaw

EDISON WATCHED IN the truck's side mirror as Jessie dropped from the flatbed and onto the dirt track, her ripe belly leading the way as she walked the length of the vehicle towards him.

He slid out from the driver's seat. "You sure you're up to this?" he asked, laying a palm on her stomach.

"Fuck, yeah," Jessie said, pushing the spade into Edison's hands and hoisting the pickaxe onto her shoulder. "That fucking cow has been keeping me awake for the last two weeks with it's braying. If Old Farmer Fuckwit ain't gonna fix it, then we will. Can't have it keeping the baby awake when it comes."

Edison grinned down at his awesome wife with a gummy smile. "C'mon then, baby. Let's fucking do this!"

***

Moonlight cut through the clouds and led the way across the cornfield to the barn at the side of the farmhouse. The cow's bellowing bounced off the buildings, and the wind whistled through the rusting harvester in the farmyard, flipping Jessie's hair around her face.

"Looks like the old bastard is asleep," Jessie said as she

peered up at the windows of the dilapidated house.

"He'll be up at five to milk them, we should get a move on."

After one last look up at the shrouded windows, Jessie pulled her holey cardigan tight across her stomach and followed her husband through the door into the barn. When she closed the door behind her, the soughing sounds of the milking machine were only just discernible above the wind.

"Jesus," Edison said, pushing his sleeve over his mouth and nose. "What the fuck is that smell?"

Gagging, Jessie stood on tiptoes to look over the nearest stall wall. Dark red patterns adorned the concrete walls and pooled on the floor beneath the festering carcass of a huge heifer, a jagged tear in its stomach leaking grisly entrails into the straw.

"What the..." Jessie breathed, eyes wide.

From deeper in the dark recesses of the barn came a forlorn lowing. "It's in the back," Edison said, and he started to make his way between stalls. Jessie followed him but stopped at the next stall, taking in the scene of gruesome devastation; a beheaded calf lying in its own juices, the docile eyes carved from its skull and nailed to the concrete wall above its head, giving a warning glare.

"Edison... I don't like this..."

Edison glanced over his shoulder as he reached the final stall. "It's in here, babe. Let's do..." His voice trailed off as his eyes adjusted to the gloom. The cow looked up at him from the bloody straw, sad eyes watering, severed legs piled neatly to one side; the black/white fur of the cow's legs and the pale, blood-streaked skin of a woman's; bright pink nail polish glinting in the meagre light.

"Fucking hell!" Edison muttered as he backed out of the stall, jumping when his shoulder touched the wall of the opposite stall.

"Help me." A quiet voice drifted to him from the other side. He stepped around it and peered into the stall. The wide eyes of a naked woman pleaded with him from the shadows, ropes binding her immobile to a bench. "Help me," she said again, barely a whisper.

The milking machine *huffed* and *swooshed* at her side.

"Holy fuck! Jess, get in here," Edison called. He rushed forwards, pulling teats from breasts—raw, bloodied nipples plopped out as the vacuum broke—just as Jessie turned the corner into the recessed area and began to scream, hands balled into fists against her lips.

"Jess! Be quiet. Call the police," Edison cried, but then his eyes moved—followed Jessie's—to where the woman's bloodied stumps, with thick black haphazard stitches criss-crossing swollen flesh where her legs had been severed, dripped bloody puss on the floor.

Back down the corridor, the barn door crashed open and loud boots stamped down the short distance. The boom of a shotgun echoed in the small space, drowning out the screams.

***

Early morning sun filtered through gaps in the wooden ceiling as Edison opened swollen eyes into the dawn of the new day. Hands nailed above his head, blood ran down his arms, pooling on his shoulders and streaking down his naked body. The sunlight stung his eyes, and he closed them again wearily.

"Jessie?" he whispered, head still foggy with confusion.

"She's a-milkin'," a voice growled from the shadows. "Quit ya yawpin' or the milk'll curdle. I got quotas to fill."

Edison's eyes snapped open, and he looked down on Jessie. Naked and attached to the milking machine, her swollen belly had deflated like a cream puff, stumps bleeding where arms and legs used to be. Next to her, the dead grey eyes of the other woman watched him as her body twitched to the rhythm of the machine.

Somewhere, not too far away, a baby cried.

Shattered

by Constantine E. Kiousis

HE'D BEEN FOLLOWING her since the pub, her silhouette outlined against the pale moonlight. She'd caught his eye immediately, her black dress and furry bucket-hat screaming "money." She wasn't bad on the eyes either. Most of those stuck-up bitches weren't.

She took a sharp turn down an alley. He grinned as he glanced around. No witnesses. Pulling a knife, he rushed down the backstreet and grabbed her, slamming her, back-first, against the wall.

Her hat fell.

His eyes widened as her hissing hair slithered and coiled.

His scream died in his throat as he fell back, shattering against the ground.

Corn Sickle Pete

by Simon Clarke

I ASK ANY newcomers to volunteer.

We celebrate the chosen person with copious amounts of cider until they pass out.

The village gathers as harvest ends with the last sheave standing. People jostle to peer into the corn for signs of life, cheer as the chosen one regains consciousness, peering through the stalks at the throng, unable to move, being buried up to their neck in the fertile soil. The final sheave must absorb nature's full potency.

The last thing they see is my curved blade flashing towards them.

They never hear the cheer as I brandish the crimson corn.

Hydra

by D. Matthew Urban

YOU GO INTO the swampland to slay the hydra.

The legends are full of information about the hydra—its venomous blood, its swarm of heads that, when sliced off, grow back double—and you've studied the legends well. You track the hydra down, cut it to bleeding chunks and burn its wounds. The venom clots. The cauterised heads stop regrowing.

What no legend told you, though, is how the swampland shifts, how its paths double back and diverge. Returning victorious, you lose your way among branching trails and your breath among poison fogs.

Your rotting flesh ripens the hydra's egg.

No More Statues

by Sophie Wagner

THE DARKNESS WAS all-consuming as he crept towards his victim, unaware that she followed closely in his footsteps. She never worried about being seen; they expected a damsel. Men never seemed to learn.

Sure, he was massive, and the broadsword in his hand was even larger. But, compared to her, he was pathetic.

With viper-like speed she lunged towards him, sinking her talons into his eyes, and pulling them from their sockets. She screamed with pure glee as he fell to his knees, clawing at his eyes.

Medusa was tired of statues. The live ones were so much more fun.

La Quintrala
and the Lord of Agony

by Ximena Escobar

CRIMSON PETALS, AS bright as the blood she spilled, did nothing to soothe their wounds. Red, like her mane swaying, as branches tore her slaves' skin and her pores wept.

She'd lain the flowers at His feet. Despite that, he still looked *down* on her. Hanging up there, on the crucifix.

No man looks at me like that in my house.

Decades later, as flames licked the eager underground and a priest returned Him home, He stretched his wooden arms at the doorway, too wide to pass.

Face up on her deathbed, mane red as hell, she pleaded to him.

The Flowering

by Jameson Grey

I 'VE ALWAYS LOVED to be loved.

I look down upon myself, endlessly gazing at my reflection in the spring, reminded of my late twin sister's beauty. Of *my* beauty.

I cannot leave now.

The air is no longer air. It has shifted—throttling my lungs as it flows through—like breathing has reversed somehow. Light-headed nausea tangles my mind, my guts.

My skin, it mottles. Bones soften, wilt. I strain toward the sun.

My feet take root. *Become* roots, drawing sustenance from below.

At this spring, I've been reborn while I watch. And although I remain Narcissus, I am flowering.

La Fee Verte

by Kimberly Rei

FROM A VERY young age, Thaddeus used whistling a jaunty tune as a means of self-comfort. Living so close to the ocean meant many late nights walking home in thick fog. Many late nights whistling. He was running out of tunes and his mouth was drying out, but until he could see more than a foot past his nose, he had no intention of stopping.

The sharply sweet scent of absinthe swirled around him, and Thad wrinkled his nose. He'd never developed a taste for the stuff. With a smell that strong, he had to be near the Wyrm. That meant being aware of more than just the fog.

It took another four steps before he realised he didn't pass the Wyrm on his way home. So where was the scent coming from?

He paused, turning in a slow circle.

His lungs collapsed, shuddered, and inflated in a panicked rush as he was slammed into a brick wall. Anise mixed with fetid ocean water, as if too many fish had died in a stagnant pool. He gagged, then forgot to breathe entirely. Blazing green eyes emerged from the haze.

Thad's heart pounded a discordant beat. Both hands

clawed frantically at the arm keeping him pressed to the wall. His shirt fell open, cut by unseen blades. No, not blades. Talons, sliding over his bare chest.

He whimpered, babbled nonsense pouring from his lips. A song rose around him, melodious and liquid. It urged him to ease. To calm. But it was too late for that.

His screams of agony pierced the night as razor-edged talons tore through his flesh. The song soared louder, riding the crests of his terror. Both went unheard.

***

The first body caused only the slightest commotion. Staff at the coroner's office joked about werewolves and if a few started surreptitiously looking over their shoulders, no one commented. The victim had been ripped open, stem to stern. That was enough to give anyone pause whilst walking to their car after hours. A betting pool had been started: animal claws or metal meat claws? Four legs or two? Which had done the deed? The pool dissolved quickly enough. There was too much work for foolish distractions. Too many bodies and too little staff.

The second and third bodies went completely unnoticed. They were found in small nearby towns where tired men simply signed the death certificates and asked the mayor-slash-undertaker to give a proper burial in the back of the cemetery, where the unknown and unpaid rested in peace. Local papers posted bear and wolf warnings. Life moved on.

The fourth body stirred some attention. An athlete, at the top of his game, found in the alley behind a sketchy little bar. He, too, was ripped wide open. The staff once more gossiped, but this time, the coroner took better notes. He took more care with the autopsy. He noticed details. He considered reaching out to other coroners, but his daughter called from college, threatening to quit. The family, the press, and the NBA all wanted a quick but flashy send-off and the coroner's notes went into a file.

The fifth body brought celebrity status and demanded answers. Or rather, her father demanded answers.

***

Maya was watching an old favourite movie, when the local station cut in with breaking news. Her initial reaction was annoyance, followed swiftly by admonishment. There had been another murder. Another?

The anchor woman was red-cheeked, eyes glittering overly bright. She was clearly in her element as she explained that this was at least the third murder, but there could be more, perhaps dozens, and the public should be terribly alarmed. News of crimes wasn't unexpected, but this story had the added thrills of being potentially serial and definitely bizarre.

"Callista Falcon, breakout star of *My Turn at Love*, and daughter of famed oil magnate Sonny Falcon, was found dead at her penthouse suite earlier tonight. Authorities aren't releasing the cause of death, but sources in the M.E.'s office say they've seen this before. We go now to Brock Daniels, on scene."

The picture cut to a perfectly coifed and tanned man holding a microphone. Behind him, a bank of police cars, light racks spinning. Beside him, a harried looking chief of police.

"Chief Garcia, what can you tell us about Miss Falcon's death? Was it suicide?"

Maya watched as the chief stiffened. He looked on the verge of punching the reporter, "At this time, I cannot release any details on the cause of death."

Before Brock could press further, the mic caught an anguished cry from off-camera, "Seawater? How the..."

Chief Garcia rushed the camera and any child up past their bedtime learned a fun new word, "Cut the fucking feed! Cut it!" The picture went blank for a split second.

The anchor team of Diane and Dane stared at the camera, then broke into matching smiles. Diane sat up a little straighter, "Well, we seem to be having technical difficulties. We'll be right back after this commercial break!"

A chill slid over Maya's skin, slow and predatory. She pulled her laptop out from under the couch and popped it open. The local news was as close to useless as you could get and still remain on the air, but it was enough to at least alert her to what she should look up. A few taps and her screen filled with a split image. On the left, Callista Falcon looked stunning on a red carpet. *My Turn at Love* was an idiot's movie, but it tickled the romcom crowd and took Callista out of soap opera status. On the right, a stretcher waited by open ambulance doors, the body bag glistening and throwing back red and blue lights.

"Hollywood Star Taken Before Her Time!" The headline screamed in bright red letters. Links to live updates, social media reactions, bios, and interviews cluttered the rest of the screen. She leaned back and closed her eyes. Seawater. Not so terribly unusual. The city was on the coast. If she opened her windows, she'd catch the scent of the ocean. She wouldn't. She didn't dare. But she could. Callista's hatred of the beach was well known. She had been quoted as saying she wouldn't be caught dead in the water.

Famous last words.

***

A long walk on the beach by moonlight. It didn't get much more cliche, but it was also a cure for nearly everything that ailed one. Cool, wet sand between the toes. A breeze off the water. The water itself, lapping at the shore. It was a temptation, of course. She wanted nothing more than to stride into the waves until she could dive and swim deep. Until she could feel the cool become cold and let the darkness wrap around her like a weighted blanket.

She knew what would happen. She wouldn't last the span of a landside day before they found her and tore her to pieces. She was wanted and not in a good way. Her people didn't have posters of fugitives. They didn't need them. They had perfect memories. Most of them.

Her memory was as tenuous as the clouds passing across the moon. It was only here, where she could smell the salt, that her mind cleared and she remembered, without confusion, who she was. What she was.

Her nostrils flared. More than salt. More than sea life. She smelled blood. Her song began to rise, smooth and sleek. It rode in on the water and caught the breeze, swirling around her. The wind rose around her and only her, and the song rose with it.

Over the years, she had tried to recreate the melody. Being exiled to the human world offered some benefits. One might even call them advantages. She had developed a love for the music created in her new home. She attended concerts and concertos, festivals and private fetes in salons. She learned to play every instrument she encountered.

None of them, not one, came close to the sounds of her youth. She managed an echo of a memory, no more. The song of her soul was beyond reach.

The rich scent of anise caught her attention and swirled around her. Hunger stirred.

A couple strolled ahead of her, hand in hand, each carrying a pair of shoes. She smiled. They were very sweet looking, heads bent together in conversation she couldn't hear. Laughter, whispers, nuzzling—all the hallmarks of love, or at least a good dose of infatuation.

The song shifted. Low tones crested over high-pitched notes, changing what was a lovely stroll to the beginning of a hunt.

She crept up behind them, following silently as they approached the pier. The structure itself was in disrepair from too many years of neglect. In its heyday, it was the place to be, with swimsuit bloomers and decorative umbrellas. Ladies rode their bicycles out over the water while gentlemen tipped their hats in greeting and admiration.

No one had ridden anything but past in decades. The dark of night conspired with the dark shadows under the wooden wharf. The water sounded different there. Waves broke against the pylons and lapped the rest of their journey rather than surged. It was a peaceful sound, one that did absolutely nothing to muffle the scream as curved talons ripped open a young man's throat. His partner, an equally young man, stumbled back and tripped over a poorly placed length of driftwood. Unfortunately for both, the pier was at the end of the beach, far from the madding crowd. No one heard the pleading. No one heard the crunching of bones as ankles, then tibia and fibular, then femur were systematically broken. She didn't mind the screeching, but she despised having to chase her meals.

***

Over the following week, three more bodies turned up. Two of them found together, broken and mangled. The

315

homeless man who discovered the young couple claimed he'd seen a beautiful and horrible woman crouched over the bodies, singing to the moon. He gave details to every news reported who would listen to him. Each time he told the tale, he embellished a little more, until all those who gave him a platform began to regret the kindness and moved along.

Still, ludicrous rumours swept across social media. Aliens, vampires, a crazy new drug on the streets that made people insane. A virus that gave people inhuman strength. That was the most popular, the most ludicrous, and the most terrifying.

The coroner's office had a leak. Word got out about the state of the dead, and no one needed to call the CDC. They swept in on their own.

Shortly after, they swept back out. There was no virus. While they agreed that the deaths were certainly unusual, they could provide no answers. By then, the public was properly wound up. The police force hired a dozen people to sit at phone banks, reassuring and taking notes. The wilder theories found their ways to websites. Details grew gorier and more salacious.

The city leaders did their best to keep the fervour to a low boil. They managed to keep the news mostly local and given the oddities, major media outlets were hesitant to report. The whole thing smacked of low-brow entertainment.

***

"Momma, she has mermaid hair!"

The declaration came from somewhere around Maya's knees. She glanced down and fell into the wide blue eyes of a young girl.

"Are you a mermaid?"

Maya crouched down, laughing gently, "No, little sister. I am not."

The girl looked sceptical. Maya held still as she reached out to stroke shimmering emerald waves, "I think you're a secret mermaid hiding from a wicked stepmother."

"Cassandra! Stop bothering the help," the shrill tones carried easily through the boutique.

Maya glanced up to see an overly made-up blonde standing at the counter. She grinned at the child, "Cassandra, is it? That is a powerful name, little sister."

The wide eyes grew wider, "It is?"

"It is. The name of a princess who could speak great truths."

"CassanDRA!"

Maya brushed fingers over the girl's cheek, then behind the shell of an ear, "Don't ever forget, okay? And don't let her see this." She opened her hand and held up a small opal stone, "A gift, from a mermaid to a princess."

Cassandra gasped, then snatched the prize and tucked it into a pocket.

The phone rang as the blonde left with her bags and a giggling child. Maya was smiling when she lifted the receiver.

"Divine Offerings, how may I help you?"

"Maya, can you close tonight? Becca's been arrested."
Samantha's voice barely masked tears and confusion.

"Tell me." Calm. Collected. On alert.

"They found a body. At the Wyrm!"

Maya held her tongue, but her calm began to waver.

"They said..." Sam stumbled as the tears began to take
hold. "They said she's the one. She's the killer."

"Well, that's just stupid, isn't it?" The reports of the
murders, both verified and speculated, ran through Maya's
mind.

"All the victims had absinthe in their system."

"That wasn't in the news," Maya forced a steady, calm
tone.

"One of those details they leave out."

"Fine, but Becca's isn't the only place to serve it." Her
head was starting to throb.

"They say it's enough to take her in."

Maya cursed softly. And in Greek.

"We can't afford a lawyer, so they stuck her with a
public defender. Maya, he can't handle this."

"One step at a time. Yes, of course I'll close. What else
do you need?"

Sam's voice shifted as she moved away from the
phone. "What? No. No! Where are you taking her? Damn it.
Maya, I'll call you. I have to go."

***

Maya leaned back in the bath. Sam's call weighed heavily on her mind. Becca was a delicate woman. She simply didn't have the strength to pull off the murders. She was all of five foot two and ran a sketchy little absinthe den, often indulging in too much of her own product. Ripping a body open, leaving the edges ragged and torn, took a sober brutality.

She shifted, seeking the solace of her favourite indulgence. The tub was deep enough to sport a built-in seat with armrests that allowed her room to stretch and flex her legs. The far wall held an array of vanilla-lotus candles, their soft light diffused by the time it reached her. Renovating the bathroom had been her first task when she acquired the apartment. It became her haven. Her home within her home.

Maya had firm rules for her bathroom. No electronics, no phones, no music, and no getting out of the tub until her toes and fingers had properly wrinkled.

She frowned and set her wineglass on the edge of the tub. She rose and grabbed a towel, soft lighting giving wet droplets an almost scale-like shimmer. There would be no peace for her tonight. The headache was getting worse.

A week later there had been no more reports of victims. Maya opened a bottle of forty-year-old Scotch and stretched out on her chaise. A large flatscreen took up most of the opposite wall. The nightly news was just starting. Two strident anchors were recapping the latest updates.

"The 'Sinthe Slayer was in court today for her bail hearing."

A screen between the anchors showed Becca, in wrist and ankle shackles, shuffling into the courtroom with the help of a very large bailiff. The dark blue jumpsuit did nothing to improve the image. The camera caught her look frantically around the room, then relax. Samantha must be there.

"Given the vile nature of these heinous murders and the Slayer's refusal to cooperate, the judge denied bail. Rebecca Sinclair will remain behind bars until the trial. And the rest of us can breathe a little easier. After the break, we'll..."

Maya muted the television and sighed. Sam had to be devastated. Becca wasn't going to be free any time soon.

After seven gruesome deaths, with absolutely nothing but the absinthe to connect them, authorities needed a win. The public was scared; the press was spinning wild tales about cults; and the mayor was sweating re-election. While many places sold absinthe, only one specialised in it. The Wyrm was a hole-in-the-wall tavern decorated in an abundance of green velvet. The pretty proprietress looked good on camera, teary-eyed and confused. Nothing remotely close to a fair trial was possible.

The questions started. How did she do it? Why did she do it? How did she choose her victims? Serial killers were supposed to have a pattern. Males in their 50s, women with brown hair who looked like Mom. But this crime spree held no pattern, and Becca could give no answers. That wouldn't save her. The death penalty was already being discussed as a sure thing. Becca was headed for the death chamber, and her lawyer wasn't smart enough to get her out of it.

The public took a deep breath, the press swarmed, and the mayor returned to glad-handing. Everyone was happy.

Maya clicked off the screen and draped an arm over her eyes.

***

The dream emerged slowly. Darkness eased in a drift of shimmering light. Cool blue water slid over her skin as she made her way towards a tangle of rocks. She pulled up on a boulder and settled into a comfortable spot, tucked against a crevice. A rush of night breeze lifted emerald hair and whipped locks around into a cloud.

She arched, savouring the salt and mist rising with each rush of water against stone. Lush lips curled in a smile as she raised a song to the full, bright moon above.

***

Maya opened Offerings with a song stuck in her head. The phone, ancient and shrill, was jangling as she flipped on the lights. Her forehead wrinkled in a wince and the song died. It was an effort to keep her voice even as she answered.

"Divine Offerings, how can I help you?"

As the day grew, so did a headache. With each ring of the phone or chime of the bell over the front door, Maya's temper frayed. By the end of the day, it took all her strength to keep from tearing into the next customer.

She was taking a last walk through the shop, straightening clothes and tidying accessories, when the bell chimed again. Fingernails bit into her palm. She painted on a smile and turned, "Good evening!"

The man looked entirely out of place as the door closed behind him. He glanced at it, panic flickering in his gaze.

Maya laughed, "Don't worry. It will open again. Just give it a good tug."

He relaxed, "I am a bit out of my depth here. I'm looking for a gift. For my daughter. She's getting married, and I wanted something…I dunno…unique?"

Maya's head flared, sending sparks of stars flashing across her vision, "Of course. A pendant, perhaps? Something she can wear on the big day?"

He nodded, eager to no longer be a lone soldier, "Exactly! Something blue, yes? That's what I read."

Her smile faltered as the pain grew. Waves and shards brought colour to the stars. Greens, blues, soft and diffused. A song wove through the pain, growing with each step she took towards her customer.

He stood in front of the jewellery display, distraught by the choices. As she stalked closer, her vision swam. Patterns of heat and energy warped around him. He was pointing to a marcasite and sapphire necklace, saying something. She couldn't hear him over the song cresting within.

***

A knock at the door startled Maya into dropping her book. She glared at it, confused by the betrayal to her solitude.

The knock came again, followed by a familiar voice, "Maya! Maya, it's Sam."

"Váll' eis kórakas!" A muttered curse, soft enough to not carry, as Maya pulled a robe over her damp, naked skin.

The smile on Sam's face made her regret her temper, "There's been another murder!"

Maya held the door open wider and let her in, lips quirking at the gasp.

"Maya! This place is"—Sam faltered, looking around with wide eyes—"amazing!"

Maya motioned to a leather couch, "Sit. Tell me what's happened."

Sam dropped herself and her bag in one motion, kicking off her shoes and tucking her legs under her. "This fabric…!"

"Sam."

"Right! Another murder. Same thing. Some middle-aged guy in the park last night. They found him strewn across a bench, ripped right open, half his guts missing."

Maya shook her head, confused. "Missing organs?"

"Mmmm. One of the few details the cops have

managed to keep out of the press."

Maya rubbed her arms, trying to not wrap them around herself. The image of the excited father blurred her vision, the tang of iron painted her senses. She ground her teeth, pretending to listen to Sam prattle about the case falling apart. Maya was falling apart. Old nightmares, long since purged, were creeping back around the edges. The headache slammed into her, then receded, taking the last wall standing with it. She knew, and she had never been more afraid.

Or more in control.

She looked up, seeing Sam through a soft glowing haze. A song gripped her throat. She dug nails into her palms, silently pleading with her nature. Sam was oblivious and her chattering wasn't helping. Maya pushed off the couch and stalked to the window. She pulled back a heavy curtain. Her nose tickled as dust snapped free. She hadn't looked through this glass since she'd moved in, hadn't been able to bear the sight.

Tears stung her eyes as her home called to her. Even in the dark, she could see the waves catch the moonlight. She could hear them breaking on the shore. The song was unbearable. She lifted her face to the dark sky and parted her lips, the rich melody of her people's power spilling free. It was time to remember.

It had been so easy, lingering outside the Wyrm, waiting for the right prey to stumble out, drunk on the forbidden. Following them, ragged lust warring with horror until the lust won out and her mind shut down. She had always fought who she was, from the moment she formed thought. Running away only brought pain. To be too far from the pull of the tide was a tense, agonizing suicide. She had found a balance at the water's edge. She thought. The father of the bride had been a mistake. They would be hunting her again, as they had for centuries.

She didn't care.

She turned slowly, the despair in her heart giving way to the hunger clawing at her throat. Sam was no longer babbling. She was watching Maya with wide, entranced eyes. Maya sang and as her tune shifted into the whisper of a night breeze, her hair flowed as if under water. Her smile became jagged, teeth razor sharp and aching for flesh. The sharp scent of anise filled the room and washed over her flicking tongue. Long slender fingers grew more so, transforming into curved talons.

She cleared the space to her friend in two steps, screeching with victory as the last glimmer of a human mask fell away. Saltwater spilled over her shoulders in a cloak trailing behind her. The ocean welcoming her back.

Sam's final words, spoken in forlorn wonder, shattered on a scream as claws ripped her chest open. "So beautiful."

***

The Spanish Coast Guard approached the compact, elite cruise ship carefully. El Sueno had been reported as out of contact twenty-four hours prior. She hadn't docked at her last port of call. There had been no radio contact, no radar tracks. There wasn't enough time for her to go far, so they found her fairly quickly based on her schedule. She wasn't much off course. But she was absolutely still.

A small craft pulled up alongside and hooked on. Two men scrambled up a side ladder, the second stumbling into the first, who had stopped cold.

The deck was slippery with blood, congealed but still wet. Chunks of what could only be flesh gleamed in the morning sun. The younger seaman leaned over the rail and lost his breakfast into the rocking sea.

"Team Two, what's your status?"

Both men ignored their radios, one because he was struggling to gain control, the other because he couldn't draw breath.

"Team Two! What is your status?" Captain Leon sounded gruff, a sure sign he was concerned. *"Dios mio, Team Two, responde!"*

It took three tries for Cabo Ramos to clear his throat enough to respond, "Mass casualties, no survivors. Send... Send...everyone."

***

Twelve nautical miles away and gaining distance, Maya raced through the water. She was far from home, far from authorities both human and her own, and completely free. Sated for the moment, she explored her new neighbourhood, singing as she broke the surface and

YEAR THREE

splashed back down, tail snapping with joy.

Bloom

by Stephanie Parent

THEY SAY THE goddess of spring was plucking a blossom when she was nabbed, yanked beneath the earth, but here's the truth: Persephone's desire made that chasm yawn wide.

Even blooming is a profession you can grow weary of; even beauty becomes a burden. Even a mother's love can twist and turn, make you boil inside till you nearly burst, till you crush the heartless petals and crack the soil.

Even darkness is a rebirth. Persephone knew this when she descended; when she went looking for jewels and fruit, deep beneath the surface, where the sun's light could never go.

Unforeseen Calamity on the Night Express

by D.J. Elton

A PULSATING CRASH awakens me, flings me across the train's carriage.

I roar. *That fool up front, he's had too much to drink.* Then I see window-side; a drooping, bloodshot eye with hairy lashes and a squint, looking at me. Frozen to the spot, craving some turps, I wet myself.

Fingers tearing into the roof. Ragged, dirty nails scurrying, scraping like an enormous spider. I'm groped and lifted out.

I come face-to-face with this evil; an enormous skeletal woman with a mouth like a Hell cavern.

She sneers, blinks, then I'm in her mouth, foul teeth starting to grind.

Ultimate Revenge

by Mike Rader

YOU'RE FIRED. I want you out of here in ten minutes."

I stared at Bill Grieve, not believing what I'd heard, and wondering why he was so precise about how long I had to clear my desk.

I'd worked at Walters, Hall & Leifitz for a decade. The advertising agency had won new business on the back of my ideas, and quite a few awards on the back of my work. But new owners had brought in Grieve as chief executive officer last year. There'd been tension in the air ever since.

"Can I ask why?" I said.

"You're a dinosaur, Joe. This agency needs new blood, young minds. Like what do you know about social media, really?" He pushed an envelope across the desk. "There's a cheque inside. Not ungenerous."

I fingered the envelope. Stared at my neatly printed name: Joe Riggio. My brain was numb. I heard a bruised voice from a fog: "Can I take my awards?"

"Agency property. Sorry, Joe." Grieve glanced at his watch. "You've got six minutes now."

Trance-like, I stalked down to my office. My face showed an unhealthy grey in the glass door. Shoved some papers into my coat, a photo of my wife and kids, and left. My secretary averted her gaze. Along the corridor nobody would meet my eyes. Grieve had them all jumpy. I passed the glass display rack in the foyer. Grabbed one of my One Show pencils. A heavy award; wanted to sink it into Grieve's skull.

I left the quaint old brownstone and headed down the street. My bank was at the intersection, where the elevated rail line divided the heritage district from the march of skyscrapers. I went in, banked the cheque, so at least I had my money. I'd need it. How many creative directors, fired in their fifties, would find a new job easily? I'd be lucky if I were hired to write copy for a catalogue company.

I crossed under the elevated rail line, stopped to catch my breath. My mind was still frozen. My chest hurt. Heartbeats boomed in my head. The truth was sinking in. I'd been fired! I hadn't seen it coming. I'd never really trusted Grieve, he was two-faced, but I thought my track record at the agency was solid. Valued. Apparently not. The new younger hungry teams would work for half my salary. I told myself maybe it was all for the best.

Glanced at my watch. Grieve's ten-minute deadline had just expired. And I was out on the street, yesterday's man. I wondered what the industry would think. Would I rate a headline in Adweek?

Suddenly my new freedom kicked in. It was time to be positive. The severance cheque would keep us afloat until I found new work. I figured I'd stop at the diner, call home, break the news, and—

Something caught my eye.

I stopped, looked back toward the agency.

Looming behind it, a block away, a huge crane worked over a construction site. Only now the giant arm was wobbling. It was like a toy. Fragile. The arm trembled again. I saw a tiny speck drop from the cabin on top and sucked in a breath.

A breathless moment later, the arm dropped like a stone.

I heard screams as passers-by saw what was happening.

Instinctively, I pressed myself back against a shop window.

Now the mighty crane tower itself tilted, trembled. In slow motion, it buckled. It came crashing toward me, vanished out of sight behind the ten-story building next to the agency.

A beat, two beats, then I heard the devastating roar as the remains of the crane struck the ground.

Silence.

I kept watching. *Oh God, no… I don't believe it!*

The building next to the agency seemed to vibrate, then sway. The entire wall facing me bulged, and an explosion of bricks came hurtling down.

I dived for the cover of the overpass. Crouched there, gaped out at the intersection, saw thousands of bricks

raining down, pounding on cars, smashing windscreens, hammering roofs flat, swallowing taxis, pulping pedestrians.

The air warped round me. Sent me rolling. An impenetrable dust cloud swirled toward me. I hurled myself to the sidewalk, felt it roll over me like a solid wave.

And when at last I finally staggered up, when I stepped back to the intersection in a daze, I saw that the agency building was lost to sight behind a mountain of rubble.

Grieve had given me ten minutes. If only he'd known.

Rise of the Hares

by Rotten Akers

"I REALLY DON'T know what to do with it, I don't decorate the room with dead animals." Crystal handed Broderick the black hare. "My publisher had this sent to me from some taxidermist they paid."

He shook his brown shaggy head of hair and grinned. "That's pretty legit, mom. Most places send a paper thing in a frame or something."

"You mean a certificate or an award?" She turned the water on over the sink and popped the dishwasher open. "I thought you'd like it better than me, maybe you could draw it for your college class."

"Yeah, that'd be perfect. Looks pretty wicked! I'm about to get good at drawing rabbits, this thing is huge."

She flinched. "Yeah. I think that's one of those jackrabbits. They're pretty nasty."

And it was. Enormous with wild fur, crooked yellow teeth, and glassy red eyes that seemed to pop. He compared it to the size of his torso—or his black lab curled up on the dog bed! Complete with whiskers that could pick up a radio signal and a gnarly, crooked ear.

Ole' dad glanced over his 'Guns an' Ammo' magazine from the bar counter. "Not a jack, but still a rodent. Good thing it's dead, I'd rather have a damned cat than a rodent in the house."

Mom wiped a plate. "Whatever kind it is, I would have shot it too."

Dad chuckled and rested his chin in hand. "I like the idea of you and a gun. And maybe camo shorts and a tube top."

Brod kept his mouth shut and side glanced at mom.

She sighed. "Yes, I'm sure. Aren't you going to be late for work?"

Dad wiped his moustache and kissed Mom on the cheek. "I'm sure I'll make it. Love you."

"Love you, too. Drive safe."

Maddie the dog watched Dad through the front door, peered back into the kitchen at the hare on the counter, and growled.

"Easy there, girl!" Brod stroked her head. "It's just a creepy dead bunny thing, it's not hurting anyone." He took the rabbit and headed for the door, "Thanks, Mom. I know a few classmates that'll totally love it."

"Brod," mom turned from the dishes. "Is everything okay with you and Shelly?"

He could feel his stomach sink. "I don't know. She's not talking to me like she used to. I think she's done."

"I'm sorry, sweetie. I liked that one." She turned to the sink again, "You'll find another one. Try not to get down too much. Have a good day, honey."

"Thanks, Mom, I'll try." He got in his car and headed off.

***

The students in the art studio broke out their gear. Portable easels, large sketch pads, charcoal, and pencils clanked and clacked throughout the room.

"We have something interesting today. We're starting with five-minute compositions." The professor tugged the sheet off the hare on the centre table, "Begin."

"Dude!" "Whoah!" "That's intense!"

Hustled sketching filled the silence.

Professor raised an eyebrow. "This is a treat from Brod. His mother didn't seem to like it, so he brought it in for us to study something unique, today. A lot easier than trying to find one that doesn't hold a pose out in the wild."

A girl moaned. "Gross."

"Gross it may be, but there's something to learn from all life." Professor smiled.

Brod had the basic shapes on his paper, ready to fill with smaller details. He glanced at Shelly, who seemed to keep her focus on the study.

She almost had a scowl under those sandy blonde bangs and was quieter than usual.

God damn it, she's still mad at me. *What did I do?* Brod kept pushing through drawing and resisted the temptation to say hello or smile at her. He didn't want to make things awkward or make the course uncomfortable because he was there.

The professor glided from behind. "Stellar work as usual, Brod. You waste no time. Keep up that practice. Very expressive, Shelly—don't forget to follow those steps, though."

Brod's glance—*Damn it! I looked!*—was met with her steel blue glare. Resistance was futile.

Shelly sneered, staring him right in the face. "Don't worry, Professor. I'll study those steps after school without any distractions." She ran her charcoal over her work with more pressure.

Brod had a knot in his chest. How could things have got so bad since the day they met here? She seemed happy to have him after their first lessons in school. Best guess: he's not welcome in her dorm anymore. *What did I do?*

***

He packed the hare under his arm and followed Shelly around the large hallway corner. "Shelly, can you at least tell me what's wrong? What did I do?"

Her backpack swayed along with her bobbing long hair in a steady march. "That's just it, Brod. That's it, right there. You have no clue."

Brod felt like he wanted to shut down, his throat was tied. He summoned his guts because she was worth it. "Help me, Shelly. I don't understand. I'll never meet someone else like you, please tell me so I can make this right."

She flipped around, the large windows illuminated her

distressed eyes into a brighter version than before. "You don't text, you don't call, you drop completely off-grid and the only time I see you for over a week is in that class."

Brod's head was running. *But isn't that enough? It's like the dates are already planned out!*

"I would think, that if I was some rare prize of a girl, I'd at least be worth some of your time. But I'm left sitting insecure and alone in my room ignoring calls from other guys because I'm waiting out on you."

He felt his stomach flip. He couldn't handle the thought of her dating someone else. This ship he put all his emotional effort into was about to sink, and if he didn't do something right now, all would be lost! "After the rest of our courses today, then. Let's go out. I can go home and study later. I can make the time—let's make a hike up to that cliffside!"

"I don't know, Brod." She faced the window. "If you wanted us to work... Wouldn't you make the time without me getting to this point?"

"I'm not doing this because you're mad at me, I'm trying to learn. I'm just an imperfect guy trying to piece this all together and do better. I'm sorry. I don't want this one to end up like the other ones, I don't know if I could handle it." He felt himself tear up, but he choked them back.

"Well, you'd better learn quick, Brod." She took off.

He had to go the other direction. "I'm sorry, Shelly. I didn't mean to do this." He wiped his eyes and put on a happy face, even though all sorts of turmoil were leaping hoops of fire through his chest. 'Well, you'd better learn quick.' What does that mean?

***

"... I was so confident in how you felt about me, I didn't know to spend more time on you. The way you'd touch me, or how your eyes light up when you see me, thrilled me like no one ever has and I got ahead of myself. You make me want to be a better person. I can only hope you'll forgive me, and I hope texting this like an emotional fool with his heart wide open won't drive you away." He tapped send and hit the bed. Only time could tell, now. Had he blown it? Was this coming to an end?

The silhouette of the hare sat in the window in front of a starlight sky. Piece after piece of art hung on his walls. He'd get lost in painting and drawing, but tonight he realised his obsession made him lose track of what was important.

The image of the hare hung up on the door. He remembered etching the details in the sketchbook while taking those glances he failed to resist, and how upset she looked. *She was hurting. And it was my fault.*

She was always so beautiful— *Did that rabbit just—*

The hare's head turned, eyes blaring like laser pointers.

Brod bolted upright in his bed, petrified in goosebumps.

Whispering broke through the room, the window, the

door... *"Crystal. Crystal. Bring me Crystal."* The voices overlapped each other.

He couldn't break eye contact with it, felt stiff, and couldn't move, as if ice-cold hands held him bound. His vision grew black until complete darkness as the whispering slowed to a stop.

He woke up, and the hare was gone. It was still night. He checked his phone, and a few hours had gone by. His eyes darted around the room. He hit the light switch. It flickered and went dark. None of the lights worked. He was in the hall when he heard it again.

"Crystal! My queen! Here she is! Crystal! Crystal!" The whispering was stronger, down the hall in his parents' bedroom.

Brod moved forward with his phone light out, turned the door handle, and pushed the door open with a long squeak. The voices grew louder.

Large black rabbits were all over his mother, pulling her lifeless body apart with little clawed hands. Her guts hung over the bed while one munched away on the entrails, others peeled off flesh, and another picked a blood-spitting eye from her socket like a vegetable in the garden.

PLOP!

"MOM, NO!!!" Brod bolted upright in bed, screaming so hard he thought his throat might rip out. It was daylight, and the hare was back in the window. His heartbeat pounded fast and heavy like a kick drum rocking away.

His mom and dad burst through his door, the ole' man up front in a bathrobe. "Good lord, boy! It sounds like you're dying in here!"

"Sweety, are you okay?" His mom rushed to the bedside.

Maddie pounced on the bed, whimpered, and put her paw on his knee.

Brod took a breath and scratched her head, "I'm good, I'm good. Just had a serious nightmare, is all. It was crazy."

His dad raised his eyebrows. "Damn straight I'd say so! I forgot to wipe and almost had a haemorrhoid, boy! Scared the shit out of me—literally!"

Mom rolled her eyes so hard, she almost didn't need a rabbit to pop them out. "World's number one most attractive man."

Dad grinned. "Thanks! I thought I was feeling mighty fine today, too, I'd say." He put a hand on his hip, "You been watching some late-night TV or something there, son?"

Brod nodded at the hare, "I think this thing might be freaking the hell out of me more than I thought. Maybe I'll see if I can leave it in the art room, today."

Mom and dad looked at each other.

"I could have sworn it was whispering your name, Mom, and it was calling you the queen or something."

Dad laughed. "Haha! Like your writing pen pal, huh, sweety?"

She grinned. "Yeah, that is something that weirdo

would have said, isn't it? But I heard he died recently. My writers' group has been saying it was a suicide."

Dad rubbed his forehead. "That's unfortunate for your friend, honey. I'm sorry to hear that."

"More like just a creep I had to work with—he made me uncomfortable. It's sad he died that way, though."

Dad turned. "Well, I'd better hustle. I'll be out of town a few days cause they're sending me to another factory. They got some staffing issues I gotta sort out."

"I'd better get back to work myself, I have a deadline soon. Are you going to be okay, sweety?"

Brod smiled. "Yeah, I'm glad it was just a dream."

"All right, don't forget that deal with your dad about you living at home during college. If he's out of town, you need to keep up on his share of the yard work."

"I got it, Mom. I'll be out in a bit."

***

Brod checked his phone on the campus walkway. Still no reply from Shelly. He blew it. She'd never bother with his stupid ass again, he was sure. He bet she'd—

What the hell?

Rabbits. Students from the art class all had a black hare they carried around campus like a pet for show and tell. Their backs were straight, the posture in their stride formal, and they cradled the bunnies like a crown for a king.

"Whoah, that's a cool-looking pet!" One student approached.

The art student gave him a blank stare and stroked the rabbit's fur.

"Can I pet him?"

"Do you like your finger?"

The student raised a brow and chuckled. "Yeah, I'd say I do. Well, cool bunny, man. See ya."

Brod ran his fingers through his hair. He halfway wondered if he was still in a nightmare but knew too well he was awake. *Something's wrong.*

None of the classmates acknowledged existence around them. No smiles, no hello, no waves. They all went single file into the art studio.

"Hey, brah." A frat boy approached Brod. "You got a dead one. What's going on in that class, man?"

Brod looked at his hare. "I guess they got inspired to get rabbits. I have no idea."

"All right, man! Have fun drawing your bunnies, that size is badass! It's like a dog!"

Brod scratched his head. "Yeah dude, sure thing."

The professor sat at the desk on the computer, head tilted to the side and grimacing. In an uncertain tone he asked, "What's going on here? This is an art course, not an FFA club."

Brod walked up, "Hey, I was wondering…could I donate this hare to the college? I'd like to leave it here in the studio, if that's alright?"

"That would be wonderful. No problem! Set it on the

shelf over there. I'll lock it in the glass case with the rest of the references."

Brod turned and gasped— "Shelly!"

She was standing in the circle of students holding a hare, stroking its fur. "You're pathetic."

He felt needles in his chest. That one hurt. But it's not like her—not even when she's mad at him would she say something to hurt his feelings...

They're being mind-controlled!

"That's not very kind, Shelly." Professor came around the desk. "Let's break out the materials."

The students stood still and looked at the professor.

"What is this, April fools?" The professor grinned with a furrowed brow. "Well, I have a nice one for you today. An aspiring bodybuilder, and an art model. Our first life study of humans. Isn't that exciting!"

The students stared.

Brod put his hand on the professor's shoulder. "Maybe we should get out of here?"

"Ha! Well, we're acting a bit strange, today. Probably a joke. I'll play along. Enter, models!"

A man and woman walked in with towels on, disrobed, and climbed onto the centre table. They looked around the room confused.

The man turned. "This is an art class—right?"

"This makes me a little uncomfortable, and I've posed for a lot of classes before. Just saying." The woman twirled her hair around her finger.

A student spoke up. "They are willing."

The others nodded.

The girl who thought the hare was gross yesterday, now holding one of her own, scratched its ear. "Feed the hoard."

The rampant pattering of many tiny paws could be heard in the hall. Black rabbits frothing at the mouth poured through the doors and swarmed the models.

Brod and the professor stepped back. Their jaws dropped.

The man and woman wailed and screamed. Blood ran down the table as they were pulled apart and eaten.

The professor broke down in tears. "Dear God, have mercy! No!"

The students watched, not even a flinch as red, goopy spatter hit their faces and clothes.

Brod took off, "Fuck this shit!" —then stopped and looked back—"Shelly! Shelly, wake up!"

No response.

The swarm turned attention to the professor.

Brod bolted. He heard the tortured screams fade as he made his way to an exit.

He got outside on his phone, "There's an infestation! Rabbits are killing people in the college!"

"We'll dispatch as soon as we can. You know there's a fine for prank calling the emergency line, right?"

"Yes, I'm aware! This isn't a prank!"

"All right, we're sending help. Calm down and stay on the line with me, let's get your name..."

Police arrived and found three dead bodies. The students went missing, along with the hares. Traces of rodent faeces were found all over.

Brod finished giving his statements and was free to go. *Where could Shelly be?*

***

He checked her dorm. Her roommates hadn't seen her. They've called, but no answer.

It was on his way home when the nosy old neighbour lady called. "I don't know what your parents are thinking adopting a colony of rabbits, but they've torn up your yard, and if they start on mine, we're going to have a problem."

"No, they didn't. They're bad, they're an infestation!" *God, no! Not the house!*

"Well, this is something I'll have to take care of myself. I have a few traps in the—"

"No, no! Those aren't good rabbits, they'll kill you! Whatever you do, don't go outside!"

"Oh, my. Is that why your dog is howling on the roof? It's disturbing the whole neighbourhood."

He floored the gas. "I'll be there in a minute!"

"Are your parents out of town?"

"Just my dad, isn't my mom there?"

"I think she would have stopped this ruckus by now if she was."

Brod's tyres squealed around the corner. The sun set over the suburb, and sure enough, there was Maddie on the roof with rabbits bouncing on the fence as they tried to pursue her.

The garbage cans were knocked down with trash all over, the garden beds were pulled apart, and the front door hung open next to a broken window.

The old neighbour lady peered from behind her curtains with a frown and furrowed brow behind her thick glasses.

Brod tried to call his mom: no answer. Then his dad: straight to voicemail. His job won't let him have his phone out on the factory floor. Brod pulled in and didn't risk getting out. The hares bounced around his car squeaking like wild cannibals.

Maddie looked from the roof with big eyes and ears down.

Brod shook. He lost his girlfriend, his home was a disaster, and there's no telling what happened to his mother. He assumed the worst, and with a burst, threw his car into reverse and stomped the pedal.

KA-THUMP KA-THUMP! The tyres screeched—

Forward drive—

BUMP! THUMP—KA-THUMP! Into the lawn—his dad would be pissed about the yard anyway—

Rear-drive—

KA-THUMP KA-THUMP!

Brod saw red. Back and forth he went, batshit crazy

rabbit guts and body parts smeared in the driveway and crippled all over the lawn.

The swarm fought back, even cracked a web in the windshield with one's face leaving a splat, but furry hide and bone was no match for steel—

BANG! The car stopped.

The hares were in a daze, rolling in pain.

Brod got out. A rabbit femur jutted through the back tyre, and the rim stuck in the dirt.

The few hares left came to and charged.

He ran into the house, shut the door, and went into his parents' bedroom. His mom was gone, and the room was torn apart. His eyes landed on dad's shotgun.

Dad showed him how to load it, how to aim it, and how to shoot it—but to "never fucking touch it."

"Sorry, dad." Brod loaded.

Glass broke in the front room, scampering came down the hall—

BLAM!

Rabbit brains hit the wall.

CHuck-CHICK! He stepped through the doorway.

A hare leaped—

BLAM!

Shredded entrails across the ceiling and carpet.

CHuck-CHICK! He marched into the front room.

Another crawled along without a bottom half as it hissed and growled.

BLAM! CHuck-CHICK!

One leaped into the window and—

BLAM!

Right through the face. Its tongue flittered bloody spit out its open skull and fell back onto the patio. PLAP!

CHuck-CHICK! He reloaded.

One more on the lawn.

Brod beat it with the butt of the gun. He smashed its legs and pinned it down by the neck, "Talk to me you little prick! I know you can! Where did you take her!?"

It hissed and clawed at him with its front paws, but no whisper. No talking. No fear.

"Fuck you!" He smashed its head.

It jittered until lifeless.

The sun went down.

Maddie howled on the roof under the moon.

He cleared his head and took a deep breath to cool down. "I'm coming, girl. I'll get you down." He headed for the garage.

Bright lights, and a siren blared from behind.

A patrol car sped diagonally into the driveway as the door popped open.

"Drop your weapon and get on the ground!" The officer approached with his pistol drawn. "Hands where I can see them!"

Brod dropped, doing as he was told. The shotgun clanked on the concrete. "Officer, hold on! They were attacking me—"

"We got a call about gunfire within city limits, which is a felony, and animal cruel— Shhhit..."—he looked over the lawn—"these rabbits."

The old neighbour lady walked up from behind the officer and adjusted her glasses. "They're so big."

"Yeah." Brod rolled his eyes.

Maddie barked.

The officer aimed his flashlight on the roof. "How the hell did the dog get up there?"

"The rabbits," Brod sighed. "They chased her up there. She leaped up by the fencing."

"Code red! Code red! Officer down in the cemetery! We need backup! Code—" The radio blared with a wail, then cut off.

"I copy that. What the—"

More of them. Their eyes glowed like diamonds in the night as they scurried over the fence. Four pairs, eight, sixteen...

"Run!" Brod grabbed his shotgun and dashed to the old lady. "We need to get you back inside!"

The officer hesitated with his pistol, aimed into the swarm, and backed into his car. *BAP! BAP! BAP!* "Oh my god, *no!*"

They pulled him apart on the ground.

His screams of agony reverberated through the street. "Shoot me! Shoot me!" Only his head was visible in the pile of black fur.

The lady fled into her door as Brod leaped from her steps, into his driveway, and—*BLAM!*

The swarm feasted.

The radio came on. *"All units advised, stay clear of the cemetery until backup arrives!"*

Brod bolted down the sidewalk.

***

He approached the iron gates past the empty squad cars with their lights on. *CHuck-CHICK!* Seven shells were left, including the four in the chamber.

An eerie green flame glowed from the centre of the cemetery. A few bloody corpses picked off, their messy bodies lay on the sidewalks near the entrance and inside the fence on the walkways.

Brod ran in behind one of the old trees near a set of tall headstones. He trembled but had nothing to lose unless he could take it all back.

Students from the art class walked around with their rabbits in one arm, and random household weapons in the other.

Shelly!

She moved along with them on patrol armed with a sledgehammer.

Whatever they were guarding at the flame had to be stopped.

He stumbled forward over an officer's dead body and

351

pulled a baton out of his hand.

One of the students armed with a screwdriver approached.

Brod hid behind a headstone and dropped his shotgun.

The student looked back and forth, the hare wiggled its nose, and they walked away.

He crept from behind—*CRACK!*—over the head with the baton.

The hare looked back—

CRACK! into its face.

It squealed and hit the ground—

Brod stomped, pinned its chest into the grass—*THUK*—and stabbed the baton through its teeth and into its mouth.

It gagged and clawed as its eyes glowed.

He grabbed the screwdriver from his knocked-out classmate—*PUK!*—right through the eye.

Footsteps. Shelly heard.

Brod dislodged the screwdriver and scrambled on the ground back behind the headstones.

She stood over the dead rabbit.

Her hare flicked its ear out and hissed, "Intruder! Search!"

The rabbit swarm poured through the fence.

Brod readied his shotgun and shuddered as they passed him.

"Imbeciles! No self-control, you pigs!"

The swarm devoured the student on the ground, now dead.

Shelly walked to the headstone. The hare in her arm looked around over top.

Brod jumped up and grabbed its head—*THUK!*

The hare dropped with the screwdriver straight up through the neck and into its brain.

Shelly readied her sledgehammer and tried to swing, but Brod tackled her into the ground too soon.

"Wake up! Wake up!"

She struggled with a scowl on her face, and her eyes turned red as she hissed.

He couldn't stand it. He did the first thing that came to his mind. "I love you!"

She almost belted a scream but fell silent and limp under passionate lip lock. A second passed, and she found herself with arms around him, pressing her kiss back.

Brod combed her hair, and a tear fell. "Shelly?"

She pouted. "I love you, too."

Brod couldn't describe how it felt to hear that from her for the first time, but time was short. "Run, get out of here. I may not see you again, but at least you know."

A rabbit in the swarm let out a squeaky burp, its eyes landed on Brod and Shelly, and the others began to come to from their feeding frenzy.

"Run!"

Shelly took off around the headstones.

BLAM!

Several hares got hit by the shot and blew their bodies open. The others still pursued.

Brod was on the run. *CHick-CHUCK! So much for sneaking it out!* But deep down, he knew Shelly was worth the risk. BLAM!

Two hares backflipped from the impact off a headstone.

CHick-CHUCK! He was getting closer to the green flame. He could see a woman in front of it.

The swarm still pursued, seven left.

BLAM! Now six. *CHick-CHUCK!* He ran another stretch. *BLAM!* Now five. Out of ammo.

The remainder gained on him.

He had to reload, but there was too much action to focus on getting the shells into the chamber. Only three left, damn it!

The taxidermy hare sat on a stool on the other side of the fire, but it wasn't dead anymore. It was fat-full of guts and breathing.

The woman was Brod's mom. She gazed into its laser eyes in a trance with a knife in hand.

"Mom!"

It sputtered drool as it chuckled. "Crystal. We can finally be together."

The 'gross' girl strode up at Brod with a baseball bat.

Her hare squeaked, "The master has declared your mother the queen. We cannot be stopped after their union!

Attack this intruder, girl!"

Gross girl hacked the bat at Brod, but her flimsy arm met with his and dropped it.

"Agh! No!" The hare leaped at him.

THUMP! The butt of the shotgun knocked it on its back.

Gross girl reached for her bat—

THUMP! Brod stomped her and picked it up instead. *KRAK!* He hit a swarm hare across the head.

It jittered in the dirt. They caught up. Four left.

"You're dead, you fool! We'll only call upon more!"

KRRANG! Brod shut it up. *KRRANG!*

Another swarm hare fell to the side.

Brod bludgeoned the others, but they were still alive. Two left. He dropped the bat and loaded the shotgun.

Other students in the cemetery looked inward on the scene as their hares wailed, and more swarms poured in.

Their eyes glistened with their bouncy hops.

The master hare laughed like a drunk. "You're so stupid, boy! Crystal, begin and be mine!"

Mom raised the knife over her wrist.

"NO!" *KRAK!* Shelly slugged the master hare across the body from behind with her sledgehammer.

"Ack!" It flew and thumped grass with a loud fart. "You fuckin' bitch!" It got up and brushed its fur off.

She struggled the knife away from Mom.

"Shelly—" Brod felt a sharp pain in his leg. "Aargh!"

The two hares dug into him with their teeth, and he fell.

Shelly screamed, "Kill it, Brod! Now!"

He took aim—*BLAM!*

A chunk came out of part of its head with the crooked ear.

The swarms and hares in the arms of students all ran away into the night.

***

Brod was near death from bleeding, but survived. He and Shelly were doing better than ever.

They cosied up in the car as other vehicles pulled into the drive-in. The drinks were cold, and the buttered popcorn was delicious.

Brod ate a piece. "I didn't know we still had drive-ins. What movie are we watching?"

Shelly shrugged. "There're a few new ones, but I forget what tonight's was supposed to be."

Brod's mom and dad were together in their truck next to them. His dad had his window down with his foot rested on the side mirror, seat kicked back, and a 'Guns N' Ammo' magazine in hand.

Everyone settled in, the lights over the field turned off, and the reel came on.

Master hare's face appeared across the big screen with a missing ear and chunk of its skull. Its single eye glowed. "Bring me Crystal!"

Dad opened his door. "Over my dead body, you fat

fuck!"

New thralls—from who knows where—walked in front of the audience holding rabbits and firearms.

Shining eyes of swarms approached behind them.

People in the surrounding vehicles froze, still in a trance.

Brod got out and yelled. "Don't look at his eye! Run! We need to get out of here!"

Shelly started the car. "Get in!"

Dad walked from behind his truck with a new assault rifle and handed Brod his old shotgun. "This time we'll do it together, son."

Spicing Up Breakfast

by Andrew Kurtz

*T*HERE'S NOTHING QUITE like adding that special ingredient to transform breakfast from dull to spectacular, Roy thought as he stood in his garden, dressed only in a bathrobe, and holding an empty glass jar.

The soil was still damp from the previous day's rainfall, which was an advantage to Roy as he squatted down.

"There you are! You're not getting away from me." Roy scooped his hand into the soil, collecting a couple of wriggling earthworms—who happened to be in the wrong place at the right time—and tossing them in the jar.

A buzzing sound reached Roy's ears, and he turned quickly, trying to find the source. A housefly struggling on a spider's web was sending vibrations across the silk, alerting a large, hairy arachnid. As the housefly fought to free itself, hirsute legs slowly approached.

Roy reached down, grabbing both the spider, fly, and part of the web. Affronted, the spider sank its fangs into Roy's soft flesh, causing beads of blood to appear.

"Son of a bitch!" Roy mumbled as he shook the insects off his hand and into the jar, a few drops of his own blood dripping in with them.

Ever since he'd eaten a bumblebee when he was ten years old—a puerile playground dare—he'd become addicted to the taste of insects.

Special ingredients sorted, Roy strolled back to his kitchen.

He took two eggs, a stick of butter, and a bag of ready-grated cheese from the refrigerator. He whisked the eggs and cheese in a cup with a fork while he waited for the butter to melt in a pan, then poured the mixture into the hot fat.

"Out of the jar and into the fire," he said as he sprinkled the contents of the jar onto the eggs as they cooked.

The worms melted into the mixture immediately, as well as the semi-conscious fly. The spider's web dissolved, and the spider—Roy liked to imagine this bit—silently screamed in excruciating agony as, first, the hairy flesh peeled away, and then it and the exoskeleton melted in to the hot eggs.

Roy used an egg slice to fold the omelette and scoop it out onto a plate, before placing it at the table and sitting down to eat.

"Ambrosia of the gods," Roy said, slowly chewing the food and savouring every morsel.

What a beautiful Sunday morning this is turning out to be, Roy thought to himself as he watched television later.

A loud knock at the door had him springing from the

couch. *Who the hell can that be at this hour on a Sunday?*

As Roy looked through the peephole and saw the morning sun seemed to have been blacked out by a cloak of darkness. *What the heck? A solar eclipse?*

Roy opened the door to a man in a long black overcoat and woollen hat. He was taller even than the seven-foot door frame, his head partly hidden in the folds of the coat.

"You gave me quite a fright," he said to the stranger. "I thought for a minute there was a solar eclipse, but it was only your coat."

Roy laughed, but the stranger remained silent. "How can I help you?" Roy asked, squinting into the sun to try to make out the stranger's face.

The stranger bent down and seemed to be sniffing him, though Roy couldn't see a nose. As the distance closed, a nauseating odour wafted at Roy, as though the stranger had rolled in a pile of shit.

"Apologies for the intrusion, but I am very distraught," the man explained. "My precious children are missing, and I have searched the entire neighbourhood. What's a poor father to do? I am at my wits' end," he continued, straightening up again.

"I am afraid that I can't help you. Have you notified the police?" Roy asked, already closing the door.

A knobbly brown stick appeared in the gap, stopping Roy from closing it.

"What are you doing?" Roy asked, panic rising. "I

already told you I can't help you. Please, just leave me alone," Roy argued.

As if he hadn't been interrupted, the man continued speaking, "The police can't help me. Perhaps my children are playing in your garden. They are very mischievous."

"There are no children in my garden! Please leave, or I will call the police." Roy was almost shouting, sweat beading on his brow. "You must understand that I can't help you!"

"All this searching has given me an appetite. Let's have breakfast and discuss this matter some more," the man said, calmly.

"No!" Roy yelled. "There are plenty of diners open— go to one of them!"

The man pulled something long from under his coat.

"I won't repeat myself again. Let's have breakfast," he insisted.

"Don't shoot! Please don't kill me!" Roy pleaded. "Of course, we can have breakfast," he said, taking a deep breath. "Come in, but please put the gun down."

The protruding object was lowered back into the folds of the overcoat.

"I can cook an omelette. Would you like that?" Roy asked, his voice trembling.

"That would be delightful."

The first two eggs Roy took out of the refrigerator slipped out of his shaking hands and smashed on the floor.

Roy cleaned them up, discarding the shells and eggy gloop in the bin, before taking two more out along with a bar of butter and preparing the omelette.

"You seem nervous. Is there something wrong?" the man asked as Roy put the plate of eggs down with shaky hands.

"I am not accustomed to doing this at gunpoint. What is it you want of me?" he asked with a tremor in his voice.

"This morning, I sensed my children playing in a garden. They were very happy, frolicking in the grass and mud. One of my children was preparing to eat his breakfast, when he was violently interrupted."

The man moved the eggs around on the plate with his fork.

"These eggs look exquisite," he said with a sniff. "But a special ingredient is needed to make them perfectly divine." The man stood and opened his overcoat—what had seemed to be an overcoat—and two large wings unravelled, revealing a torso and eight spindly brown legs.

The hat slipped off and a cockroach's head with two long antennae were unveiled.

Roy gasped, mouth open. "That was no stick in the door, and you don't have a gun!" Sudden realisation fuelled his bravery. "My, you're definitely a big one. I bet you taste delicious. I'm sure you're aware of my predilection for creatures—I'll enjoy eating you for lunch, covered in hot, melted cheese." Roy salivated, and picking up a kitchen knife from the counter, he approached the insect.

Roy lifted his arm and was about to stab the creature in the chest, when a long brown spindly leg whipped out and pierced Roy's skull.

Roy's face froze; an eternal look of horror etched on his face.

The cockroach peered into Roy's dead eyes. "Just as you enjoyed the taste of my children, I am going to enjoy eating you." The cockroach violently tore Roy's head from his body, laughing maniacally laughed. Blood gushed from the headless corpse's neck as it collapsed on the floor, a thick crimson pool spreading out beneath it.

The cockroach brought Roy's head closer to its mandibles and began to strip off chunks of flesh, rapidly chewing each tiny morsel. Roy's eyes were gouged out, and a viscous, black liquid dripped down his cheek. A gory mix of brain matter and blood smeared the roach's face as it noisily sucked out Roy's brain.

When it was finished, all that remained was a picked-clean, fleshless skull.

Very tasty, but a bit dry, the roach chirruped with satisfaction.

It opened the front door and tucked the skull under its huge wing. *I'll keep this as a souvenir.*

"What a beautiful Sunday morning this is turning out to be," the roach whispered before spreading its wings and lifting into the clear blue sky.

Finally Over

by Evan Baughfman

CRIMSON LIGHTS FLICKERED along twisted strands, causing the tall tree to resemble a creature with blinking red eyes. Ghoulish garland snaked across countertops, cluttered with holiday cheer. The fireplace roared with hellish flames. Stockings hung limp, like fresh corpses from the gallows.

Aghast, I turned to my wife, shrieking, "No! What did you *do*?" My voice drowned beneath carols blaring from stereo speakers.

Cobwebs had been replaced with tinsel... Skeletons exchanged for elves... Jack-o'-lanterns ousted for Santa's eerie visage!

"Halloween's finally over," said my wife, sipping cocoa through a peppermint straw.

I moaned. "But Christmas already...? It's only November first!"

One Sacrifice Demands Another

by C.L. Sidell

THE TREE WAS too big for our house; its crown bent under the ceiling and too-long branches snatched our sleeves when we walked past.

"Best find in the state!" Pops boasted.

We woke Christmas morning to find every present under the tree open, a red-eyed ghoul crouched among wrapping paper and pine needles.

"No good," it hissed, fangs bared. "I require greater compensation"—it scratched the trunk—"for losing home."

Pops scanned the room. Then, finger shaking, pointed at me.

"You can have *him*."

A scream clawed at my throat as Pops slunk backward, and the creature, salivating, slowly approached.

Naughty and Nice

by Pauline Yates

ON CHRISTMAS MORNING, I wake to find a blonde and a brunette, naked as newborn babes, asleep in our bed. They fit the description written on my husband's Christmas wish list. He wished for a threesome—without me.

Wondering if Santa granted my Christmas wish, I hurry downstairs to the Christmas tree. I clap my hands with joy. My husband is impaled on the trunk, with red baubles jammed in his eyes, his intestines strung out like tinsel, and his Christmas wish list shoved up his…

Nice. Serves him right, unfaithful bastard. I must send Santa a thank you note.

Red Wrapping Paper

by D. Matthew Urban

DECEMBER 24, 11:54 p.m. Not yet.
I stand over my baby brother's crib.

December 24, 11:55 p.m. Not yet.
He's sleeping. So innocent.

December 24, 11:56 p.m. Not yet.
I never thought I'd have a baby brother.

December 24, 11:57 p.m. Not yet.
I thought it'd be just me and Mom, forever.

December 24, 11:58 p.m. Not yet.
"My miracle," Mom said. "My present from heaven."

December 24, 11:59 p.m. Not yet.
Almost time. I raise my arm, hold the knife high.

December 25, 12:00 a.m.
Christmas morning. Time to open the present.

Season of Giving

by Brianna Witte

ISNATCHED UP the large present under the Christmas tree, the bright red wrapping paper dropping to the ground in shreds. I opened the white box, my little heart racing with excitement. My breath caught, the pure astonishment paralysing me.

A human head sat perfectly preserved in the bag; the dark blood accumulated at the bottom reminding me of the fresh meat lining the grocery aisle. The face of my fourth-grade bully stared back at me, his mouth open and eyes wide. I jumped up in excitement, gleefully hugging my dad.

"I love it! This is the best Christmas ever!"

Maybe Next Year

by Sophie Wagner

WHAT DO YOU think, Stephen? Have we been good this year?"

"For his sake," he said, "let's hope so."

Santa lay spread eagle atop a pile of coal, held in place by candy canes that were shoved through his forearms, his one remaining eye still twinkling.

Walter scanned both lists, then shook his head sadly. "Another year, another Christmas on the naughty list. Care to guess what we won?"

He grabbed Santa's sack and shook another pound of coal onto the pile.

"Such a shame," said Stephen, pouring lighting fluid over the pyre and striking a match. "Maybe next year?"

It's Beginning to Look a Lot like Christmas

by Simon Clarke

CHRISTMAS TOMORROW, WE need to make space for the family. They had planned a move to Australia; I blamed our son, Mary blamed our daughter-in-law. We would never see the grandchildren again. It wasn't fair. We'd be just another lonely, miserable old couple, despite all our years of help and support.

It's funny how if you think about something long enough, anything is possible. So we prepared, went on an adult education course, "Taxidermy for the Family". Anyway, I think we should get them out early this year, so they are sitting round the table when we get up tomorrow.

Spam Christmas

by W. Ed George

GERMANS HERALD THE Holy Child with breads, pickles and wurst. "Yummy," decrees my mother-in-law from Dusseldorf each year; I call it "Spam Christmas."

She takes umbrage; injects politics, money, *my* drinking every time. Holidays thus ratchet our rivalry.

But this year I've set the menu. I'll mince garlic till our kitchen stinks, baste fatty shoulder (two) and slather on the Morton's Tender Quick. *Voila*, Spam Christmas!

"Mum woulda loved this," *mein liebster* will gush. "Sad she stayed home."

I'll confess on Boxing Day how, after much badgering, his mother *had* graced our yuletide table—rendered, uncharacteristically silent, and tastefully dressed.

Santa Baby

by Lindsey Harrington

S HE LICKS HER lips and surveys his upside-down, unconscious face. Sugarplum eyes to shuck, button nose to bite off, and bowed lips that will twist and stretch with each procedure, his *Ho-Ho-Ows* bouncing off the decorated walls.

She pauses and frowns. *Is the prey too easy?* Her smirk returns. *Nah!* Serves the fat bastard right for rushing headlong down her chimney.

The laws of physics warned him that he'd get stuck eventually. But the man in red thought the rules didn't apply to him. And it's fate, not physics, that trapped him here.

Santa's delivered his last piece of coal.

Daddy's Little Girl

by Blaise Langlois

THE NOTE, PROPPED up against a plate of cookies, read: *For Santa*. No persuasion was required—Saint Nick had come to expect such delicacies. After washing down the treats with a tall glass of milk, he wiped his mouth with the back of his hand. He considered the remaining crumbs but doubled over in agony, as a searing pain tore through his abdomen. A foul stench erupted from him and he projectile vomited, covering himself and the floor in Christmas red. Behind the chair, the young girl smiled as "I Caught Mommy Kissing Santa Claus" played softly in the background.

Into Every Life Falls a Little Rain, Dear

by Steven Holding

TIS GOODWILL SEASON, and the Devil's fuming.

Despite different addresses (one red-hot, another ice cold), post destined for the pole keeps appearing. Incorrect grammar's the reason: lists from mixed-up kids who can't spell S-A-N-T-A. Both wear red, keep company with knee-high entities, but there the similarities end.

Sickened, Old Nick's quick to teach Saint Nick a lesson: Christmas isn't white, but crimson.

Come the twenty-fifth, he's found the sleigh, sniggering "Naughty *or* nice, everyone's due a surprise. Something shocking in their stocking—not Jingle bells, but Hell's bells and buckets of blood!"

Hidden in Santa's bed—nine severed reindeer heads.

The Naughty List

by Les Talma

S HE MADE A deal with Santa.

It was uncommon, but she had been very good, while others had been very bad.

So bad that they'd driven her best friend to suicide with cruel taunts and ceaseless torments.

Coal just wouldn't cut it.

But now, she'd be punishing those naughty-listers. Just her, them, a toolbox full of sharpened candy canes, a sturdy hammer, some Christmas lights, and maybe some black ops elves to help…

After this, she'd never be on the nice list again.

She was fine with that.

And when she was done, she'd have some gloriously screaming Christmas displays.

Santa's Stockings

by Jonathan Worlde

SANTA USED HIS elf power to contort his body, sliding his way down the Grinch's chimney. He had a devious surprise for that narcissistic monster who hated children and Christmas cheer.

Santa delicately inserted a cylinder containing super-volatile nitroglycerin into the Grinch's stocking. Come morning, when the Grinch opened the surprise, the world would be free of the pathological bully.

Turning to scramble back up the chimney, Santa's coat button caught on the stocking's fabric. The cylinder jostled against the fireplace brick, immediately imploding. Santa juice was blasted up the chimney, across the rooftop, fatty muck landing on Rudolph's nose.

Down the Chimney

by Jameson Grey

HE'S HERE!" I half-whispered into the walkie-talkie. "On my say-so, you know what to do."

I was watching the roof from the treehouse in the back yard, bundled up against the frigid December night. A rotund, red-suited figure was squeezing into the chimney.

I shimmied along the branch, eased myself onto the house's flat roof and tiptoed swiftly over to the chimney. Hearing grunts of effort from within, I replaced the cap I'd taken off earlier.

"Light it up!" I yelled.

"Got him!" crackled the response, followed by fiery screams from below.

My brother and I had always hated Christmas.

Merry Christmas

by Matt Hawkers

FACE GLEAMING AND bright, ruddy shades illuminating his cheeks, Alex blew on his hands and stomped his feet to stave off the cold.

In the upstairs windows his wife and children waved their hands in time with a soundless tune, their mouths open wide.

Oranges twinkled in his eyes as he watched the fingers of flames dance; watched the faces of his loved ones melt away to nothing.

Red and white throbbing lights and high-pitched tumultuous wails turned his street into a rave.

Alex grinned as he gave himself up—at least there'd be no bloody socks for Christmas anymore.

Frau Perchta

by S. Jade Path

I JUST DON'T know what to do anymore! Vandalism!" Luka's mum wept bitterly. "He used to be such a *good* child."

***

Luka slammed the door, kicking it for good measure.

So unfair! Grounded over Christmas break! The paint will wash off...

Throwing himself onto the bed in his pique, he quickly fell asleep, worn out by the day's dramatics.

***

Luka woke screaming, his tummy burning. Looking down, he saw his entrails spilt over the duvet like a grisly Christmas garland. Luka watched in dread fascination, blood loss darkening his vision, as Frau Perchta started stuffing straw into his now-emptied belly.

Happy New Year from Iceland

by Avery Hunter

In Icelandic, Nýr means New, and Gamall means Old.

Be kind to one another in 2022 and beyond. Unless you walk in another's shoes, never underestimate the darkness they're trying to manage.

NÝR'S EYES SPARKLE in the streetlights as she watches the woman stumble from the nightclub, drink-sodden Happy-New-Years echoing down the street in her wake.

"Hello, again," she says, and the young woman looks up, a flash of recognition widening her smile.

"I thought you'd never come," Gamall whispers.

Nýr grins and takes Gamall's hand, leading her into the shadows.

Nýr leans her against the wall, pressing their bodies together, and strokes stray hair from Gamall's neck before gently placing a kiss there.

Gamall shivers in anticipation, a quiet moan escaping.

Licking a long stroke with her tongue, scraping the skin with her fangs, Nýr smiles as she lovingly pinches the skin with her lips before slowly sinking her teeth into the soft

flesh.

Gamall shudders in her arms, breathes a "Thank fuck."

Gamall tearily kisses her brief lover goodbye and groans with her final breath, "It's been a crazy year; I'm glad it's over. Take care, Nýr."

Nýr carefully lays her old friend on the ground, before turning and dancing away to her new life.

Black Hare Press

BLACK HARE PRESS is a small, independent publisher based in Melbourne, Australia.

Founded in 2018, our aim has always been to champion emerging authors from all around the globe and offer opportunities for them to participate in speculative fiction and horror short story anthologies.

Connect: linktr.ee/blackharepress